To

Fred

ENTANGLED
IN TERROR

Entangled in Terror

Published by The Conrad Press Ltd. in the United Kingdom 2023

Tel: +44(0)1227 472 874
www.theconradpress.com
info@theconradpress.com

ISBN 978-1-914913-81-5

Copyright © Fred Titchener, 2023

Printed and bound in Great Britain by Clays Ltd, Elcograf S.p.A

Typesetting and cover design by The Book Typesetters
www.thebooktypesetters.com

The Conrad Press logo was designed by Maria Priestley.

ENTANGLED IN TERROR

Fred Titchener

Chapter 1

كُن قويًا لأجلك

Stay strong for yourself.

A perfect blue sky set off a ragged line of hills which bordered a flat desert landscape.

The wind whipped up the sand into the air as if brushed by an invisible broom. A small boy crouched out in the open, stroking a thin mangy dog which laid on its back staring up into the boy's face with appreciative eyes.

The boy's house was just over a road, from open desert, it was adjacent to a storehouse which had been taken from the boy's family in the name of Islam. A man, his head covered by a red and white chequered scarf sat against the door, every so often his head nodded forward, his eyes closing as the heat led him into slumber.

Across his lap lay an AK47 loosely held in his hands. The boy looked at him in disgust as the dog yawned.

Suddenly the dog stiffened and looked towards the hills,

the boy's eyes followed the dog's gaze. Two small specks appeared low over the hills and sped swiftly down over the rocks dropping lower and lower till just above the desert plain, ever onward they came towards the boy. The dog growled and looked to the boy for comfort, he responded stroking his head and whispering to him.

The noise of the jets suddenly caught up with their progress materialising into a roar as they screeched over the village, causing the man to wake, and stare in puzzlement, as they banked away heading back to the line of hills. The man resumed his slumber. The dog slid away from the boy and trotted over to an outcrop of rocks, watched by the boy until he realised the planes were circling back towards them. He rose and quickly joined the dog in the shelter of the rocks.

The jets continued on their previous path towards the storehouse, low and straight, each spitting out a black missile with a glowing tail. The man dropped his rifle in horror as the realisation struck him. The missiles hit the storehouse, erupting in flames, this was followed by a huge explosion. A fierce wind blew over the sheltering boy hugging his dog. The noise of the explosion was followed by a rain of falling debris. Then, for what seemed an eternity a number of smaller explosions followed as if from a gun battle, and then, there was total silence as the dust cleared. The boy poked his head over the rocks and mouthed the one word, 'mother.'

The storehouse, which was his home, and the surrounding houses lay flattened in a tangle of broken masonry heaped up in piles, spreading onto the road, where a sole car alarm registered a noisy protest from its smouldering carcass. The boy stared in stunned silence, mixed with the terrible realisation of his fate. He knew instantly, he had joined the ranks of so many other orphans, and was alone.

Several minutes elapsed before other villagers emerged from semi-collapsed buildings peppered with holes from the exploding ammunition. They appeared as ghosts, covered in a light-coloured dust with faces already streaked with tears. Soft moans emanated from a woman cradled in the arms of a husband, and another young boy crawled from the ruins of his house, his 'Superman' T-shirt ripped and blooded.

A young girl, her eyes wide and her face streaked with tears embraced the boy. 'Your house is gone, mother, sister gone too?'

'Yes Amira, all gone.'

They stood together looking helpless at the scene slowly coming to life with villagers searching in the rubble for relatives and friends. An open truck drew up and a man got out carrying a pistol in one hand. He stared at the devastation and cursed, seeing the boy he demanded.

'Where is Abdullah?'

The boy still clutching the girl close whispered.

'You sacrificed my mother and sister for your bullets and guns.'

The man waved the gun impatiently.

'They died to glorify Allah, boy.'

The dog growled and bared its teeth as the man spat on the ground. The boy freed himself from the girl and held the dog, watching the pistol, before moving slowly away, followed by the dog. The girl ran a few steps and spoke.

'Habib, where are you going?'

'To my uncle, there is nothing left here for me, Amira.'

The man moved to stop him, but the dog rounded on him and let out a deep growl. He cursed again and spat on the ground, but did not pursue the boy as he walked slowly away from the scene of horror. The man belonged to a militia group who had taken the storehouse owned by the family, and used it to store weapons and explosives. The family had been prevented from leaving their home, which was built adjacent to their business. His mother realising the obvious danger they would be in, protested, but was told it was all in the name of Allah. She had replied that it would be them, the militia, which would answer to Allah come the judgement day, as they were not doing the sacrifice but making others do it for them.

The girl ran after the boy handing him a bottle of water she had been holding, and gently kissed him. As he walked away silently, she waved tiny fingers. The man walked over to where the group's ammunition dump had been and kicked at the ground. In the distance they could hear sirens coming closer. He jumped in the truck and drove past the boy in a cloud of dust and away down the road.

The boy continued without breaking step, the dog at his heels, in the direction of his uncle's house further down the Beqaa Valley towards Nabatiyeh and the Israeli border. Just outside the village he collected the family's four goats. The sad little group proceeded along the old paths parallel to the road, away from the militias, keeping the Lebanon Mountains to their right, way in the distance. The boy knew enough of the desert to be able to forage for food and water and with the goats he had enough to sustain him, and the dog, for the eight days it took him to walk to his uncle's house.

His aunt met him and greeted him with great relief having heard the news of the Israeli Air Force's strike on the militia's armoury, and the death of her sister and niece. She hugged the boy surrounded by the goats and the dog, which collapsed on the earth in apparent exhaustion.

'You are safe now, Habib,' she said, 'we will take care of you. How did you get the animals here too, it's a miracle?' He at last broke down and wept in his aunt's arms as the dog rose and snuggled up to him, licking his tears as he bent to stroke it.

The uncle and aunt were in their middle age, their children long gone to forge their own lives in Beirut. They had a tiny small-holding, swelled now by the addition of the goats. The house was small, but they found a space for Habib and his dog.

Habib stayed with his uncle and aunt for several months doing odd jobs about the house and tending the goats. He rarely spoke, and had recurrent nightmares, which alarmed his aunt.

'A boy of his age should not have had to suffer such an ordeal; he never speaks of his mother or sister. His father already a martyr too. I am so worried he will follow the path of so many other boys in his position. The militias target such as him. Habib is a gentle, good boy, and deserves a good life.'

There was another uncle who lived in London, and he

had heard of the events in the Lebanon, but did not realise that Habib had survived, until his brother contacted him. He asked after the boy and when he was told by his sister-in-law of her fears for him, he decided to offer him a home in London away from the troubles of the Middle East.

Habib was now fourteen years old, he knew nothing of the modern world away from the Lebanon and it filled him with wonder, confusion and strangely a degree of comfort. His new uncle, who he had never met, was a kindly middle-aged man who ran his own carpet import business. He lived in a large terraced house in west London with an elderly housekeeper. The uncle was not a devout Muslim, and was duly horrified by the story he coaxed out of the boy. The housekeeper immediately took to Habib and became a surrogate mother to him.

He was a quiet boy who took his school studies seriously, and soon learnt enough English to take school exams. He formed a friendship with an English boy who was similarly quiet and studious which set them apart from the rest of the English children. The teachers at the school, knowing his background, were amazed at his capacity to learn, and his application, and took great trouble to see he got every opportunity. His friend's father ran a small electronics company manufacturing security devices, and Habib became fascinated by the field of electronics. He carried this interest into the world of physics, and with good grades in the sixth form was awarded a place at a university in London reading electronic engineering.

It was a cruel twist of fate that found Habib sharing a flat with a group of students from the London School of

Economics, who were looking for a romantic cause to champion, and they had decided to support the Palestinian struggle for an independent state. Habib was irritated by their interest in things he felt did not concern them, and he told them that they did not fully understand either the history or the politics. At first, he refused to be drawn into their discussions on the subject. He kept telling them that they had no idea of the suffering imposed on the ordinary Arab caught between the Israelis and the hard-line Palestinian factions, and advised them not to get involved.

In London, the Palestinian Liberation Organisation leaders were due to meet representatives from the Israeli government, as part of the continuation of the 'Camp David' talks. The students, two boys and a girl, were part of a left-wing group within the LSE, intent on joining a demonstration against Israeli attacks in Southern Lebanon and the annexation of Arab land in order to build more Kibbutz. The demonstration had been fixed to coincide with the meeting.

The girl tried to get Habib to join in the march, but he told her that he had a new life now away from the terror and evil that marred his childhood. She got him to tell his story, and he recounted how the militia used his family as a human shield to protect their arsenal. The girl was insistent that the Israelis delivered the air strike in the full knowledge of the situation, regardless of the innocent lives that inevitably would be lost, and that he was abandoning the Arab cause by his indifference.

'Look the militia leaders are only interested in power and money,' insisted Habib. 'There is as much fighting between the various factions as there is against Israel, if you go on the march, you will be demonstrating against the PLO, who at least, are looking for a peaceful solution to the problem now,' insisted Habib.

'But they must hold out for a Palestinian State, free of Israel,' countered the girl. 'They must not surrender, and become a puppet state within Israel. I am not sure that is the PLO's agenda, their leader's just want to protect their own comfortable lives.'

The girl's name was Hilda, she was from a well to do family, and her grandmother had been a friend of the Bloomsbury Group of free thinkers, a rebellious trait indelibly etched in her DNA.

Her boyfriend Pete was the second son of a lord who was clearly looking for a romantic adventure. He had taken every opportunity to rebel against a strict upbringing in the shadow of his brother, who had been groomed to continue a dynasty going back to before the Middle Ages.

The third flat member was Roderick, he was from a different background altogether. He was the son of a Welsh miner, brought up in a strong socialist environment. As a lad, he had sold the Socialist Worker newspaper on street corners in Cardiff and London, and had been arrested several times for breach of the peace and assault on Police. He had used his supposed deprived background to get a place at the LSE and was determined to promote his social-ist views. He was a cunning individual, who was prepared to use his friendship with the couple of 'romantics' to further a career in politics, and above all make money.

Roderick immediately saw Habib as someone who could

be used as a focal point for promoting their cause, an asset directly connected to the cause through his suffering. He kept telling him he was turning his back on his Arab heritage and Islam. This annoyed Habib, who said they were just playing with political ideology, in the full knowledge, that if they got their fingers burnt, they could go back to a comfortable existence in British society, he had no such option.

'I have a new life here, I am not being shot at or blown up, and I don't wish to put my career at risk, my uncle has sacrificed much to get me to university, if I get into trouble, I would be just slapping him in the face,' said Habib with feeling, tinged with annoyance.

Hilda tried desperately to get him to come and just listen to the speakers, as she felt he would change his mind about the realities of the situation now, as he had been away from the Middle East for some time.

'We have Arab friends who have been through similar hardship and events to you, they are more passionate now, than they ever were, and want to make a real statement of support for the Palestinian cause, the Arab cause, your cause.'

'Ok, go, demonstrate,' Habib replied, clearly irritated. 'See what good it will do. You just want a flag to wave, I am staying here, I have work to do, and that is what you should be doing. Go, try to get yourself in a position where your voice will be heard, by those who can make a real difference. What do you think, seriously, that you will achieve by all this?'

'We will make a statement that will be heard, in

solidarity with our Palestinian friends, together, our voice will be heard,' added Roderick.

'Be careful: these people, who say they are your brothers, could just be using you,' warned Habib.

'If you don't want to fight for your people. I will,' Roderick announced with some fervour. The trio had been preparing all manner of banners and with these tucked under their arms they went off to demonstrate.

The march started peacefully with the usual groups of demonstrators carrying placards and banners, most of which were homemade and carried a slogan advocating a 'Palestinian Free State,' others in the march were supporting a variety of left wing causes from 'Gay Rights against Rage' to 'Save the Whale.'

A line of bored policeman flanked the march whose head was quite tightly bunched and then fell away into a loose straggle, which included elderly people, some on walking frames, and young mums pushing infants in pushchairs. The atmosphere was good humoured with sporadic chants of 'Free Palestine,' and 'No to Israeli Puppet State.' The procession wound its prearranged course through central London until an 'El Al' bus was spotted in a side street. The march faltered and most marchers stopped. The chants grew louder with fingers pointed at the bus.

The police line moved up to cover the street as best it could, and a Policeman tried to get the bus to move. A group of more militant demonstrators broke through the thin line of police and attacked the bus as passengers attempted to board. There was an exchange of words between the people on the bus and the angry mob as airline staff pushed their passengers into the bus.

Hussein Mustafa, a well-known and respected Palestinian moderate was spotted sitting in the bus. A couple of demonstrators banged on the window where he sat trying to remain calm and dignified. Suddenly a man, with a scarf over his face, produced a handgun and forced his way onto the bus and fired a shot at the diplomat.

An armed Israeli sky-marshal in the hotel doorway promptly pulled his gun, forced his way through the crowd and shot at the gunman. Excited demonstrators still kept attacking the bus as the wounded gunman fled from the scene. All hell broke loose with confused marchers screaming, some attacked the Israeli security man, and generally got in the way of the police. A small group enveloped the gunman as he ran away down an alleyway mews followed by other demonstrators, one of whom was Roderick. Some of the demonstrators who had not heard the shots above the general hullabaloo, wrestled with Police as they tried to secure the bus and give medical aid to the shot diplomat. The gunman who was supported by two friends, was bundled into a waiting car. The fleeing gunman and his rescuers seemed disorientated by events and Roderick shouted to them.

'Go through the arch, the yard opens at the other end.'

'Come!' yelled one of the men.

Roderick was pushed into the car, with the gunman, by his friend, who shouted.

'Show me!'

The car whipped through the yard under Roderick's

guidance and out into a parallel street empty of traffic and sped away unnoticed by the crowd or police reinforcements arriving.

'We need to see to his wounds, have you a place where we can do that?' asked one of the men.

Roderick said 'yes' and directed them to his flat saying he would be safe there while they attended to him. The gunman had a slight flesh wound to his chest but was bleeding profusely.

'But you can't stay there for any length of time,' said Roderick.

'Who will be at the flat?'

'The other students are on the demonstration, except for an Arab student, but it would be best not to involve him,' said Roderick.

They half-carried Hassan the gunman up to Roderick's room, as quietly as they could so as not to disturb Habib. There they tried to stem the flow of blood, but Hassan was getting progressively weaker. They made a call to the Mosque, where another member of their group was alerted to their plight. This man found a sympathetic medical student who rushed to the flat and duly removed the bullet and bandaged the wound.

Habib by now had heard all the frantic comings and goings and asked Roderick what was going on. Irritated by the enquiry and still excited by events Roderick said, 'keep away, or you will be in trouble with the police, or my friends, if you get in the way.'

Habib could see blood on the stair rail and quickly retreated to his room and locked the door.

A short while later Hilda and Pete returned to the flat to find the wounded Hassan, Asif his friend, and the medical student. They wanted Hassan moved as soon as possible out of the flat. The medical student agreed it would be wise, he said his patient was stable and could be moved. Asif knew a safe house they could go to out of London, but they would need some form of vehicle to transport Hassan. Pete said his father 's firm had Transit vans which were not too far away, and he could get one for them, if they agreed to move Hassan out of the flat directly.

Pete ran the distance to the open yard where the vehicles were housed. The watchman was initially unwilling to let him take a van, but knowing he was the boss's son eventually agreed to let him use a van providing he returned it before he went off shift. Pete drove the van straight round to the flat and Hassan was walked down the steps of the house and put into the van where he was laid on blankets in the rear. Roderick volunteered to drive the van with Asif and the medical student looking after the wounded Hassan. He reassured Pete he would return directly, once Hassan had been safely deposited.

The car used to get the gunman from the shooting to the flat sat in the road outside the students flat. The Israeli Sky Marshal had got a partial number of the vehicle, and this had been circulated to all units of the Metropolitan Police. A local police officer later saw the car parked, and when he looked through the window, he saw bloodstains on the rear seats. The local collator identified Roderick as a resident of the flat opposite and pointed out he was a known left-wing militant with a history of violence. The PC was instructed to maintain a watch on the vehicle and this he did from an adjacent flat as the Anti-Terrorist Branch assembled a team supplemented with firearms officers.

The PC said that there had been no movement from the house or anyone going near the vehicle while he watched. An Anti-Terrorist Branch officer duly knocked on the door and gained entry, followed immediately by firearms officers who quickly secured all the flats.

Traces of blood were seen on the furniture in the flat belonging to Roderick. Hilda and Pete were immediately arrested in connection with the shooting. They were extremely vociferous in their denial of any wrongdoing, and initially denied being at the demonstration, until a placard was found in the kitchen. Habib was arrested too, and told the officers he had been in his flat all afternoon and had not been anywhere near the demonstration. The bloodstains were pointed out to the students, who immediately said they were not responsible for them being there, and had no idea how they got there. The flat clearly was used by Roderick and when asked about him, they all said they had not seen him, and did not know where he was.

Roderick, meanwhile, had driven Hassan to a small farmhouse in the Hertfordshire countryside, and after depositing the three Arabs he took the van back to Pete's father's yard. He cleaned the rear of the van and dumped the blankets, used as a bed for Hassan, in a rubbish bin. He then returned to the flat, but on seeing the police vehicles and the ATB Forensic Team outside, he hastily got out of the area.

The student's flats were in a narrow two-storey terraced

house, squeezed into a row of three storey Victorian terraced houses. There were four bedrooms off a wide landing on the upper floor with a bathroom. Each bedroom had been assigned to a particular student, to double as a study and retreat. The ground floor had a reception room, large kitchen, utility room and an extra toilet, which were for communal use. The layout was ideal for four students sharing.

The occupants of Hilda's, Pete's and Roderick's rooms provided plenty of evidence in support of the Palestinian cause. Habib's room had many documents in Arabic which were seized for translation. His desk showed evidence that he had been studying with a part drafted thesis, and other documents and study material from the university. All three were arrested.

The car outside was wrapped in plastic sheet and was taken away on a low loader vehicle for forensic examination in a controlled environment. Blood from the gunman together with Roderick's fingerprints and those of other unidentified suspects were found in the car, together with fibres matching the clothes of men seen at the demonstration, images of whom were captured on CCTV cameras in the street. The gunman's blood was also found on the stair rail as well as in Roderick's flat. No traces of blood were found in the other student's flats.

As the evidence was being processed the Palestinian Diplomat Hussein Mustafa died in hospital. There was worldwide condemnation for the atrocity together with tributes to a 'Palestinian Dove' who had been in the forefront of brokering peace in the Middle East. He was reported as a gentle man respected by both Palestinian and Israeli alike. The shooting was immediately claimed by 'The Fist of Islam Group' as the death of an enemy of 'Free Palestine,' and a traitor to Islam.

Habib, Hilda, and Pete remained in custody and Habib's uncle and housekeeper were also arrested and their house searched. Roderick was put on a 'Most wanted List' and his face appeared on the front pages of daily newspapers, the following day. Hilda and Pete's parents secured the services of established lawyers who pressured for their release.

Roderick, on leaving the outside of the flat had covered as much of his face as he could under a 'hoodie' and slipped down into Highbury and Islington underground station. He returned to the safe house of the group to find that it was empty and had been cleaned. He spent the evening scanning the TV news reports for details of the shooting. Initially he had not been identified, but he had the presence of mind to purchase hair dye to disguise his red hair, and he shaved off a small beard. He had been at the house two days waiting for the group, when he saw his face on TV. The car used in the shooting was also featured, having been stolen earlier from Edmonton.

He searched the house and eventually found a phone number, which he phoned from a phone box in the nearby village. The man who answered had a foreign accent, so Roderick identified himself and said he needed help. After an initial silence, the voice told him to stay where he was and call the same number from the phone box in two days, when he would be told what to do.

Habib, Hilda, and Pete all faced hours of questions.

Hilda and Pete conceded they had both been at the demonstration but were nowhere near the coach when the shooting took place, a fact confirmed by the CCTV tapes of the incident. They also denied being in the house when the gunman was brought there and had alibis to cover the material period. Habib denied being at the demonstration and no trace of him was found on any of the surveillance tapes. He said he had heard much coming and going at the flat when the gunman had been there, and he insisted he had locked his door, kept inside his room, and had no idea what had been going on. At the LSE students held a sit-in in support of Hilda and Pete, demanding their release.

The identity of the three students held in connection with the incident appeared in the newspapers and the watchman at Pete's father's yard told police of the circumstances surrounding the borrowing of the van and its return by Roderick. However, the van had been used by several other employees of the firm in the interim period, which limited the forensic recovery. Pete said he took the van for Roderick, but did not know what it was really going to be used for.

Habib's uncle and housekeeper were released and immediately arranged legal representation for Habib, but his uncle said that he did not want to see him again if he was released. All three students were later informed by their legal representatives that they could face charges of harbouring a fugitive and possibly conspiracy to murder as a worst-case scenario. Habib was told that police had intelligence that his family had housed a terrorist arsenal until it was blown up by the Israeli Air Force. Habib reacted furiously:

'The militia used my family, and our neighbours, as a human shield, they stole my father's business and store-house, for their arsenal, it was my family, my mother, my sister, who were killed by the Israeli jets, they did not care who they killed. My mother, my sister, they were not ter-rorists. I have forged a new life here, away from all this viol-ence, I am innocent of all of this. You will not find any proof of my involvement in their demonstration, or that shooting. I was studying at the flat. I wanted them to leave me alone, and let me finish my studies. I had no interest in their activities.'

Then, suddenly, all three were released. At the UCL Habib was told that the principal was considering his future at the university. It had been suggested that his skills as an electronics engineer could be useful to a terrorist group, and he should take care not to get involved in Middle East politics. He immediately went to see his tutor who had been impressed by the quality of his work, and the devotion he showed to his studies.

What Habib did not know was Professor Randall's birth name was Rakonavitz, and that he was a Jew. The Professor said he had a friend, a lawyer who was an expert in cases of deportation and international law. He had mentioned Habib's predicament to him, and the lawyer had showed great sympathy towards Habib's situation, and for the ter-rible start he had had in life, and praised his resilience. It was just obvious to him that Habib was in the wrong place at the wrong time, and it was unfortunate for him that he had fallen in with that particular group of students, who just happened to be in the flat that his uncle had found for him. He agreed with the Professor that he would have an uphill struggle when any application to remain in the UK came up. The major obstacle to any successful defence in any deportation case, would be convincing Special Branch and immigration, that he was not part of the group he found himself with. The first thing would be to show he had a supportive family behind him. The lawyer, who he referred to as Michael, would prepare papers for court and speak to the Immigration Department.

Two days later Michael contacted Habib and told him he had convinced his uncle that he was innocent of the events surrounding his arrest, and that his uncle was prepared to support his application to remain in the UK and continue his studies. He, with the support of his tutor had also convinced the university authorities that he should recommence his studies. Habib said he was so grateful to Michael and Professor Randall for what they had done on his behalf, and for turning things around so quickly.

It was then Michael said he had had some problems with the Special Branch, and their support came at a price. They wanted Habib to return to the flat, to Hilda and Pete. He was not to get involved in their politics and maintain the stance he had originally adopted with respect to their support of Palestinian sovereignty. In the first instance he did not want Habib to contact them directly, but to use his tutor as a go between. He was to tell Professor Randall if Roderick or anyone of Middle Eastern origin got in contact with his flatmates, and that was all. Above all he was not get involved and not discuss with them the arrangement they had.

Habib said that he was reluctant to take on the role of an informant. Michael emphasised that all he was expected to do was to keep his tutor informed and keep a low profile. He said he fully understood his reluctance, which was natural, and that he should make any call from a phone box outside the house where the flat was, and, above all he was not to put himself at risk or have his current life compromised by any action he took. He told him he could discuss it with his uncle if he had any doubts about the arrangement, but with no one else.

'However, if you run into any serious problems, do not hesitate to contact me, and come to me first, as your lawyer. Here is a contact phone number where I can be reached, twenty-four hours a day. Do this, and the authorities will be kindly disposed towards your predicament, and I feel sure, they will allow you to remain here,' said Michael, laying a reassuring hand on Habib's arm.

Habib went directly to his uncle to thank him for taking him back into the fold of the family, and to ask his advice about the proposition Michael had made to him. His uncle, as a foreign national would have been under similar scrutiny following his own arrest in the incident, and was only too willing to comply with any request by the authorities for help, in order to save his business and current way of life in the UK. What the uncle or Habib would not have known was, who those authorities really were. So, his uncle advised Habib, that on balance, he felt Habib should do what Michael, his lawyer, suggested.

'After all it is just to make a phone call,' said his uncle. 'You owe those other students nothing, as they put you in this awful position in the first place.'

So, Habib returned to the flat, to Hilda and Pete. Michael had insisted that it would not be a good idea to ask the couple directly for any information, just in case they became suspicious of his motives. Hilda and Pete welcomed him back, saying he was very fortunate to be allowed to stay.

Pete said, 'I am surprised, that you as an Arab, were not just kicked out as being involved with desperate terrorists, like us, they must be getting soft.'

Habib replied that he had not done anything and had never supported their crackpot ideas, and this was blatantly obvious to the police. He added that his stance on their politics had not changed, and he still did not wish to be involved, he only wished to continue his studies in peace.

Hilda and Pete after a short period of non-involvement in the Palestinian cause were soon attending meetings again, and joined in another protest in Parliament Square, for the Palestinian cause. They talked freely in front of Habib, and on occasions tried to drag him into the debates, but he still remained distant advising them not to get involved in matters that did not concern them.

Two weeks later Michael contacted Habib at the university to find out how he had settled back in the flat with Hilda and Pete, and whether there were any problems. He had taken Habib to a café where the meeting was relaxed. Michael seemed more concerned that Habib had not encountered any awkwardness with the couple. He did not ask any direct questions about their activities, or about Roderick, and added that all was going well with respect to the question of deportation, which, as a threat had now become less of a concern. The support of the university and his tutor had been crucial and the total lack of evidence to connect him with the shooting and any pro-Palestinian activity had helped, but he must continue with their arrangement, at least for the present.

It was only a week later, when Hilda let slip in conversation that Roderick had been back in touch. He had told her that he was safe and was protected by the group. It was apparent to Habib that she did not know where Roderick or the group were. Habib told her that she would be stupid to get involved with him again, to which she replied that the Palestinian cause was a just one and that if decent people did not act it was a poor state of affairs. A world run by the big powers and their puppets was one that she did not wish to be part of.

Habib somewhat reluctantly contacted his tutor as arranged and passed on the information. Michael duly contacted him and arranged a meeting at the café near UCL for that day. He asked Habib to be extra vigilant as he felt Roderick may ask his friends to do something stupid which may jeopardise their whole futures. If Roderick came to the house, he was not to engage him in any way but contact Michael as soon as it was clear to do so. It would be essential, that he could prove later that he had never been involved in their activities, or with Roderick. Michael said that he would take any action necessary with respect to the authorities.

Back at the flat Hilda and Pete seemed excited about undisclosed developments. They did not reveal to Habib what was happening, and he warned them again not to get involved. Roderick had up to that point been staying at a safe house used by the group and soon discovered that they were the infamous 'Fist of Islam.' In the early hours of one morning, they woke Roderick and told him that it was not safe for him to remain at that address as he could well compromise it, and they had a safer place for him to stay where he could 'embrace Islam' and become a true believer in solidarity against Israel and the west.

The building, he was driven to, was in a complex close to a mosque set deep in the countryside. There he met more members of the group who said that he must, like them, keep a low profile, as the general members of the mosque did not appreciate, or know, what they were doing.

Roderick was reassured that he would be safe at this 'retreat' as the police were reluctant to search the premises, because of the political fallout, that would inevitably result. They told him that if he really wanted to help their cause he must convert to Islam. Feeling that he did not have any alternative, he agreed to do just that. He was told he must show humility, embrace the Koran and the teachings as he would have to convince the Imam he was genuine. The Imam was initially suspicious of the new follower, but after a lecture, Roderick started his studies, and joined in at daily prayers and made sure the Imam saw that he took his devotions seriously.

After prayers one evening members of the group, now known to him as Abou, Abdullah and Magib showed him an 'anarchist cookbook' written in English. They told him it has been copied from a US Special Forces Field Manual which had been designed to instruct militia groups opposed to Islam. Abou asked him to interpret some of the more complex written passages and diagrams and they then explored the idea of making simple incendiary devices from innocent household items. Roderick quickly suspected that they were testing his resolve and establish how far he would be prepared to go, so he played along.

The Imam had been watching Roderick closely and confronted him telling him he now knew he was a 'wanted man' and was unhappy about his presence within the protection of the mosque. He told him further that he suspected the little group he was associating with were up to no good. Roderick insisted he just wished to be converted to Islam and was sympathetic to the Palestinian cause and nothing else. He had no idea what his friends long term aims were. This did not convince the Imam, so he summoned Roderick's friends together and lectured them that Roderick was not a true convert, that he was just another adventurer who would not stay true to the faith. He pointed out to them that a free Palestine could only be achieved through prayer and diplomacy and not through violence, and that in the Koran there was no mention of what they called Jihad.

'What you are doing is not the will of Allah. Why do you involve this boy in Palestinian affairs? You are once again bringing trouble to the mosque; you will leave as soon as is practicable, and take all your belongings with you,' the Imam said in forceful tones.

Abou responded saying they were truly engaged in a

Holy Jihad against Israel and the US and Roderick had a moral obligation to help them as they had given him sanctuary. They insisted that he had become a true convert, that he had been treated badly as a youth by his country's authorities, and now Islam and the true faith offered him a new way of life.

'You should be glad he is studying the Koran, and comes to prayers. You are obliged to give him, and us, shelter,' said Abou.

'If it means compromising the house of Allah, the answer is no, now get out,' said the Imam quietly, but firmly.

Abdullah then launched into a torrent of Arabic, waving his arms frantically, until the group was suddenly surrounded by young men offering protection to the Imam. The group made a tactical withdrawal taking Roderick with them. Abdullah was still muttering under his breath, as the group held a conference in Arabic. Roderick was told to collect his things and be ready to leave. Abou left and made a phone call at the first telephone box he came to. When he returned, he told the group they were to leave. They got into their car and drove off towards the Midlands.

Eventually they stopped at a ramshackle farmhouse where they were met by a strange 'hippy' woman who hugged Abou. It became apparent that she had at some time been a girlfriend and was keen to rekindle their relationship. She was delighted they were going to stay for a few days.

The farm's main building was little more than a whitewashed cottage with a number of semi derelict outbuildings dotted around. It was set at the end of a narrow track invisible from the main road behind a copse. A few chickens were running free outside the front door, and an old border collie made a token effort to bark as the group approach from the car, which was later driven into one of the barns. Abou said he would stay with the girl in her room, and the rest of the group were to take over a room at the rear of the cottage, where mattresses were provided on the floor. The farm had once been a hippy commune, but the former residents had all drifted away back to civilisation. The girl was given money to get more supplies and food from the village shop, and they all settled down to plan their next move.

Next day out in the barn Abou got Roderick to help him with experiments to make the simple incendiary mixtures shown in the book he had seen at the mosque. Small quantities of the mixture were made up from items the girl had at the farm. The chemical formula was one that resulted in a particularly volatile and friction sensitive combination, which when tested flared and burnt violently.

'Of course, we'll need significant quantities of these chemicals later, if we wish to make any impact, on the forthcoming peace talks,' Abou told Roderick.

'If a number of these low-key devices are set off, where they can just make a noise, it will at least draw attention to the depth of feeling for the cause. The police and the press, will blow the situation out of all proportion, and we will achieve publicity, good or bad, it does not matter,' said Abou. 'What we need are larger quantities of the chemicals, they are, as you can see harmless substances.'

Roderick was asked if he could approach his student friends to buy the chemicals involved, so as to distance the group from the purchases, the cash needed would be provided. Each chemical is an innocent item, so he was told to instruct them to buy each one from a different shop, so as not to attract any attention, or provide a clue as to their possible final use. Abou felt sure they would not realise what they were for.

'Just do not give them any indication, tell them they are wanted back in Palestine as there is a shortage there. Tell them anything,' said Abou. 'You cannot buy them, as there is a danger you could be recognised. Just tell them to collect them at the flat, and we will arrange for them to be brought to us for shipment. Of course, once they are with us, we can mix them.'

Roderick was shown a number of small timers with electronic circuit boards set in resin, and he was told that they would provide the delay mechanism. Magib told him later these timers have been made by our electronic engineer back in Lebanon. 'They are sealed units, fool proof and easy to use, the delay is marked on each. To make bombs, we only need batteries and a simple igniter, which we have. We will show you how to assemble them, and they will go in sweet boxes, so they can be placed in West End shops just before they close.'

Roderick said that he was impressed by their organisation and attention to detail, but expressed fears, that what they were about to do, would put him in very real danger of being put away for life if he was caught. Magib assured him they would look after him, as they had done so far, and that there were some very powerful people behind what they were doing, who would also protect him. As long, as he was careful, there was no real danger. He was also warned that he was in too deep and that he would face even more problems, if he were to back out.

'These incendiaries will be a diversion to keep the police busy, and their attention diverted from the main operation,' adds Abou who had assumed leadership of the group. 'They could be placed by your friends too. There must be no trace back to us, Allah has more important jobs for us to do that are far riskier.'

Roderick duly phoned Hilda and provides her with a shopping list. She is initially confused but seeing the items are harmless, is happy to oblige. Pete wonders why they are given instructions to carry out the purchases at separate shops, but he too, seeing they are harmless items, does not make any connection, and since they have not been asked to do anything with the items, he too is willing to comply, especially as the cash to cover the purchases is also provided.

At the flat Habib sees a large bottle of one of the purchased chemicals and wonders why Hilda wants such a large amount. He also sees a shopping list that Hilda has written out and the instruction to buy separately, and he then knows exactly what they are up to.

He confronts Hilda, who is not aware he has seen the list.

'Why have you bought this chemical in such quantities, surely, you cannot use this amount?'

'I have bought it for a friend. There is a shortage in their region. It will be taken away soon, so don't worry about it,' she says.

'Roderick has been back in touch, hasn't he?' said Habib.

'No, why do you say that?' said Hilda rather impatiently.

'Hilda you are about to turn the corner into full on terrorism, if you don't stop now; can't you see he is just using you, you could end up in prison for a long time.'

'Oh, come on Habib, this stuff is harmless, don't be ridiculous.'

'In isolation yes, but I am sure if you combine what he has asked you to get, you could produce something that is anything but harmless. I am pretty sure this is an incendiary mix, isn't it?' asked a clearly worried Habib.

'Come on Habib you see a terrorist around every corner, you are getting paranoid now. This stuff is in every household's cupboard,' said Hilda.

'Is Roderick coming here?' demanded Habib.

'I don't know, and I would not tell you if he was,' snapped Hilda.

Habib told her she was bound to be watched because of her connection with Roderick and she must be doubly careful not to take any risks or do anything stupid.

'If the Police see what you are buying, they will descend on this place again, and you will have to answer awkward questions, at the very least,' he said.

Habib was now very worried, and he phoned Michael directly and said what was on the list.

'God, that is an explosive mix, we have seen this stuff in many devices deployed in Israel, it is very dangerous, not only when used, but also when it is being made up.'

Habib tells him that neither Hilda nor Pete would be capable of any form of complex chemistry as they had problems making omelettes.

'Tell me if they get all the chemicals on that list, and then get out. We will handle things from then on,' said Michael.

'Do you think Roderick, or one of that group, will collect the chemicals from them?' asked Habib, with a note of caution in his voice.

'Maybe but they could try and make the explosive there, so they must be stopped,' replied Michael.

'Michael you're not just a lawyer, are you?'

'Habib, I will not do the stopping, that will be the Special Branch. Trust me, I have your interests at heart, after all, I represent you.'

'But Hilda and Pete could be hurt, they are stupid, but they are not terrorists, they are being used,' said Habib anxiously.

'Habib just tell me when they get more of the chemicals, and if they are contacted by Roderick, and we'll take it from there, don't get involved any further than you have to, you've been given another chance in life, take it.'

Habib returned to the flat and pleaded with Hilda to stop buying the chemicals on the list. She said she knew what she was doing, and she was not doing anything wrong, and he should mind his own business. Habib told her he did not want to get mixed up with them again and he was going to stay with his uncle away from them. She told him to keep quiet about all that he had seen, as there were people who would not understand.

Outside the flat, a little down the road from them, an unmarked van with no windows in its side parked up, it would routinely be replaced by another similar vehicle, the occupants of the van, were not Special Branch.

When Hilda and Pete left the house to go to college, two young men entered the house and went to the students flat. They were dressed in overalls and carried a toolbox, and to anyone seeing them they were simply maintenance men. One produced a copied key, and quickly gained entry. Inside they photographed the chemicals already purchased, and then placed tiny electronic devices before leaving, as quickly and quietly as they had entered. They, like the occupants of the van, were not Special Branch.

Chapter 2

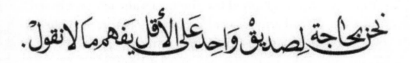

We need at least one friend who understands what we do not say.

In Belfast a young boy sits on the low wall at the front of his house, a dog sits under the boy's swinging legs. It is a plain red brick terraced house, a mirror image of the house opposite. Just down the street there is a junction with another street constructed in the same manner. The end house of the terrace has a blank wall on which has been painted a mural. The image is of a man holding a Kalashnikov rifle in one hand, and a ballot paper in the other. The backdrop is of the Irish tricolour set in a setting sun with a dove on the wing, an olive branch in its beak.

A grey armoured land rover turns into the street and slowly moves down towards the boy, he slips to the pavement and picks up a pebble. As the Land Rover passes him, he throws the pebble making it bounce off the armour. The vehicle sounds it horn. The dog barks and advances at the retreating vehicle which does not alter its speed or direction. The boy's mother comes out of the house and scolds the boy.

A man rounds the corner of the street, and the vehicle slows and stops beside him. Words are exchanged between the driver of the vehicle and the man, all in apparent good humour. The man is the boy's uncle, he is also a well-known Irish Republican and suspected Provisional IRA member. He is known within his immediate circle as Uncle Sean. He continues on down the road to the boy's house, passes the boy and opens the gate, as he does, he pauses.

'If you want to dent a 'pig' Rory you will have to throw a larger stone than that one.' He says with a straight face.

'Next time it will be a brick Uncle Sean,' the boy says with a grin.

'You'll do no such thing Rory,' scolds his mother 'don't encourage him Sean, haven't we got plenty enough troubles already. There are enough stupid idiots in this family, without you encouraging Rory to join them.'

'Is your da home, Rory?' asks Sean apparently ignoring the boy's mother. 'He is just making a statement against the forces of occupation Bridget.'

The lad runs through the doorway and shouts inside,

'Uncle Sean is here, da.'

Sean ducks, and enters a small dark parlour and before the boy can follow him, he closes the door. The room looks as though it was decorated in the Victorian era, and has never moved on. The bulb in a plain lampshade is dull giving the scene a distinctly Dickensian feel. In a high-backed chair sits the boy's father, a stocky man with black curly hair and a big round face. He looks up as Sean, a giant of a man, enters the room. Neither man smiles.

'Is the car ready, Seamus,' asks Sean.

'Yes, it's ready to go, it's in the barn with a full tank,' answers Seamus, as if the vehicle is to be used on a family trip.

'It has to be in place by one thirty. Colm knows where to take it, does he?'

'It's all set,' says Seamus, nodding his head.

'Right send him,' says Sean curtly.

'The call is due at one forty-five,' says Seamus looking instinctively at his watch.

'Ok, should give him enough time to get away then,' says Sean as he breathes in and tenses his enormous frame.

At one forty-five that afternoon a warning call is made that a bomb will go off outside the Strabane Street Army Post. Fifteen minutes later a car bomb does in fact explode at the location shattering the windows of the shops opposite. A chorus of vehicle alarms follow, as the cloud of dust clears.

As the dust settles, a number of pedestrians emerge from nowhere and hurry away from the scene. Two army land rovers screech to a halt and soldiers deploy down the street. RUC officers follow shortly after, and set up cordons across the street, a good distance from the wrecked smoking car.

The vehicle has false registration plates but is later identified as one stolen a week before. A CCTV camera has caught one of Sean's sons Declan stealing the car. A raid is carried out at Sean's house, and he is arrested along with one of his sons, ironically not the one who stole the car. As the two are being put in the car a shot rings out and a soldier in attendance standing by his Land Rover is shot and wounded.

A follow up operation the next morning sees the army and police raiding a number of properties including Seamus's house, and he and his wife are arrested. Rory is also detained, but breaks free of the policeman holding him and runs from the house, and is shot and injured. Bridget is distraught, and a scuffle breaks out witnessed by the local residents. She is dragged screaming into a Police van, and taken away as Rory is placed in an ambulance. As the story of the raid unfolds in the press, an angry mob gathers at the local RUC station. They are protesting against the shooting of young Rory, and demanding an investigation into the Army's action. The protest continues for days in the Irish press and abroad with demonstrations in North London and Boston, USA.

Rory's cousin Declan, Sean's other son, is eventually seen by police walking down the Falls Road and is arrested. He is questioned and told that police have evidence he stole the car, and is shown the CCTV footage. He says nothing, and no evidence is found that he was actively engaged in planting the bomb, as the vehicle theft had occurred a week before. He is charged with taking and driving away a motor vehicle. Some days later the RUC's enquiries lead them to the barn where the bomb car was prepared. Traces of improvised explosive are found together with the finger-prints of Seamus and Colm. Rory's father, Seamus, is duly charged with causing the explosion, but Colm is still at large, on the run. The protests at Rory's shooting duly subside and run out of steam a few days later, and are consigned to the annals of the 'troubles.'

Seamus's wife Bridget is released, and she returns home to care for the injured Rory, who is traumatised by the events. He becomes withdrawn and aggressive, particularly towards his mother and is a real problem at school. Uncle Sean is the only one who can get through to him, and recognises that he is angry and wants to vent his anger in the form of revenge. Sean sits the boy down and tells him, that he understands what is going on in his head, that the best way to strike back is to study hard at school, go to university and get qualified as an electronic engineer so he can make a real contribution.

Uncle Sean takes over the role as Rory's father, and keeps him away from the active PIRA scene. Rory's attitude gradually changes towards his mother, and he becomes quite protective towards her, understanding more of what she must be going through trying to raise a family with her husband, still in prison. However, he is still sullen and withdrawn but throws himself into his studies, gets good grades at school and gets a place in a technical college studying communications and electrical engineering.

As far as the RUC are concerned Rory has left the IRA scene despite the rest of his family being still heavily involved. At college he meets a girl and his obsession to strike back at the Army wanes. However, fate struck again. Colm, Rory's cousin, had become a notorious gunman hunted throughout the province, and is suspected of the murder of an RUC Officer. He is spotted talking to Rory and his girlfriend by two soldiers in the street where Rory's girlfriend lived.

As the soldiers approach Colm, he twists his body falling towards the ground with his hand going to his coat pocket. The soldiers immediately open fire hitting Colm and Rory's girlfriend Kathleen. She later dies in hospital.

For weeks there was a public outcry in Ireland and the wider world. Colm was found to have a handgun in his pocket, but it was not loaded. The debate as to whether he was trying to hand it over raged for weeks. Eventually he was charged with possession of a firearm, and other offences relating to its use, including the murder of an RUC officer.

Rory attended his girlfriend's funeral but said nothing throughout the service and left before it was over. He was followed from the funeral by Donal a PIRA hard liner.

'I want a few minutes of your time Rory; you have expertise we are looking for, as so many good men have been taken from us. Here is a phone number, if you are with us, call me,' says Donal quietly.

Uncle Sean had seen the meeting, and knew instantly why Donal had approached Rory.

'Rory, it's your decision, but bear in mind, we are getting close to a political solution to all this. No number of bombs or dead soldiers, is going to bring Kathleen back, but a political solution will bring justice, you are on the moral high ground now, and you can use that to great effect,' says Sean. 'The decision is yours, think on it.' Rory just nodded and went away.

The Republican press accused the British Government of Kathleen's murder. The RUC made repeated attempts to get Rory to make a statement concerning the incident, but he refused to say a word. He was advised that it was in his best interests to co-operate, which just hardened his resolve to look for ways to avenge her death.

Rory phoned Donal, and a meeting was arranged. He was asked if he wished to join the Real IRA and play a more active part in the 'struggle.' Rory agreed as he had seen enough, and was ready to find his own form of justice.

'Good man you are, just act normally, don't get involved in anything, and we will be in touch, have some clothes packed ready,' said Donal.

A few days later, in the early evening a man appeared at the door.

'Right get your clothes, we'll go now.'

His mother just watched and under her breath said, 'no Rory, no, I can't lose you too.'

'Are you ready, or not,' the man said gruffly.

'I am ready' was Rory's reply.

In the car the man asked, 'what did you tell her?'

'Nothing, but she will guess,' said Rory.

They drove through the night along dark country lanes. Rory had no idea where they were going, but guessed it was across the border. Eventually they stopped at a small farm-house. Inside it had obviously been lived in and was clean, the kitchen table was well scrubbed, an old Welsh dresser held a selection of plates and there were floral curtains across the windows.

'Ok, this is it, there is food in the fridge, and the bed

upstairs will be made. Tomorrow an old couple will come and join you. Listen to what they say, concentrate on all they say and show you. Don't waste our time, if you want to stay alive.'

With that the man left and drove off into the night. The farm cottage was all he said it was and Rory found there were clean sheets and blankets on a bed, so he went to sleep, for what was the remainder of the night.

The old couple did not come the following day or the next and Rory began to ration his food. He did not stray from the farm, which was set in rolling hills and fields separated by dry stone walls. There were no animals in the fields close to the farmhouse. Two barns and a stable made up the outbuildings. Inside one of the barns were steel drums and farm equipment, all seemed orderly and was well maintained.

On the third day an elderly couple suddenly appeared, the lady refilled the fridge with food and milk saying nothing, and the man just stood in the centre of the kitchen and stared at Rory, as if sizing him up. Rory greeted them politely.

'You realize you are giving your life for the cause boy,' he said in a gruff voice.

'Yes,' said Rory.

'You will do what you are told, listen to what I tell you.'

Rory just nodded feeling a little irritated.

'If I don't like you, I will leave, you will not waste my time, I assure you,' warned the man.

'Look I have been through a lot in my life, so let us get on with this,' snapped Rory.

'It's ok lad, relax, I do know your history, but I have to be sure you understand the position you are in, we'll start in the morning, so get some rest, that is, after the wife has made us something to eat.'

They had a plate of tasty mutton stew, mixed with chopped vegetables, eaten for the most part in silence. Rory went to the bed, he had already selected in the smaller of the bedrooms, and fell asleep quickly.

In the morning the old man, who refused to give any form of name, showed Rory some drawings of a variety of improvised devices of standard PIRA technology. He produced a number of props, all hidden in the drums, from around the barn. It was here, the first lesson in basic bomb making took place. He went slowly and methodically through a set of routines emphasising the safety features on each device. He made Rory write down the basic routines so he would understand, and would remember them.

The process took most of the day, and when they had finished, they ate a hearty wholesome meal prepared by his wife. She totally ignored Rory and hardly spoke a word to her husband either. As soon as the meal was over, they went to bed leaving Rory to stare at the wall.

The following day the course of instruction was repeated, with the old man questioning Rory at each stage. Rory learnt quickly and the old man seemed to be pleased. This was the PIRA basic explosive course, and Rory was told they might require him to take two more advanced courses later. In the evening after the meal the couple collected all their belongings, hid the instruction posters back in the drums, and left, telling Rory to remain at the farm.

It was dark when another man came and collected Rory and drove him back to his home.

'I don't have to tell you, that your little jaunt out into the countryside never happened, do I, Rory?' he said with menace in his voice.

His mother hugged Rory when he entered the house and shed a tear, but she said nothing about his trip. Uncle Sean came round in the evening.

'Everything ok, son?' he asked.

'Yes, it's fine, Uncle Sean.'

Nothing else was said on the subject. A week later another man came to the house.

'Rory you're a lucky boy, we've got you a job at a communication repair shop. They've no idea what you are really there for, and must never know.'

Rory looked puzzled 'Thank you, I was getting bored, and Mum could do with some spare cash.'

'We know you have the theory, but it will be good for you, to get some hands-on experience of some of the equipment, we want you to make and maintain. A good deal of the technical problems we encounter, are with the commercial items that we use. Fault finding on that equipment will give you valuable experience, and we hope it will lead to some innovation, as we have to modify the electronics we use all the time,' the man said, smiling.

'Sounds interesting,' replied Rory.

'While you're with the firm, keep a low profile, and don't hint at all, as to what the end game is, is that clear.'

'It is, yes,' said Rory.

'When we think you have the skills we are looking for,

we will contact you again, but until then just forget you know us, is that ok?'

For the next six months Rory mended walkie-talkie sets, timed photographic equipment, and was even involved in designing circuitry for a number of industrial projects. He worked hard and was respected for the knowledge he gained at college and his obvious expertise. His fellow workers could see he was a loner, a bit of an introvert, with an air of sadness about him and they never quizzed him about his private life. His mother was happy that he was employed in legitimate employment and appeared content, though she was conscious that the death of Kathleen, his girlfriend, was still on his mind.

One day after work, a car drew up as he walked home, and the driver told him to get in the car.

'Sean will speak to your ma; you are going for another ride. We want you to meet someone, and discuss drawings of equipment we are thinking of using in the future. The fellow you will meet, is in the same line of work as yourself.'

Once again, he was driven through the countryside and over the border winding through narrow country lanes to yet another isolated farmhouse.

At the house, another young man was waiting, he was obviously a skilled electronics engineer with a good theoretical knowledge. He told Rory he had a degree in physics from the NIHE in Dublin and was doing a masters in electronic engineering. He had been told, like Rory, not to talk about his private life.

They were there to study some drawings of sophisticated

46

remote-control devices devised by an expert based abroad. Their job was to see which ideas could be turned into effective weapon systems, at least on paper. The following day the pair allowed their creative juices to flow and eventually drew up a series of viable schemes, that looked practical from a construction standpoint, and took into account the availability of component parts that could be purchased in Ireland or from standard electronic mail order sources.

They stayed at the house overnight, and worked through the following day, refining their choice of devices, and drawing up the relevant circuit diagrams, adding a list of the components to be mounted on them. The diagrams included timing circuitry for short delays of a few hours, and long delays of several days. They were relatively simple circuits, however they made use of some integrated circuits that had just arrived on the commercial market. In addition, some simple remote-control devices with coded circuits, were also devised together with a few more complex mechanisms, for firing multiple rockets.

As darkness descended on the farmhouse the lads relaxed with a couple of beers they had found in the fridge. It was not long before a car arrived for Rory's new friend, who had given his name as Danny, to take him back to the Dublin area. Danny had, like Rory, been briefed not to give details of where he was from. As Danny was driven off, Rory's driver arrived and took him back through the winding roads to Belfast.

Rory's life resumed its normal course at the workshop for the next month. Then one evening he was again collected on his way home from work, and driven off through the Armagh countryside and over the border to the same farmhouse as he had been with Danny. However, this time he was met by an older man, who told him that they had got all the materials he and Danny had listed, and there were all the tools he would require as well.

The man then began to outline which of the circuits he wanted Rory to produce, and the quantity required. He gave him a list, which he told him to destroy once the devices were constructed and tested. An oscilloscope and other testing rigs were found in sealed boxes, concealed under hay in one of the barns. He then showed Rory where he was to store the items he produced. These would be sealed in waterproof bags and put back in the boxes along with all the tools he used, these were then all to be placed in a concealed bunker for future use.

The bunker could be accessed from a drain cover in one of the outhouses, which had been used as a cowshed, the cover was at the bottom of a dirty trough where there was a layer of cows muck. The cover once removed, revealed a set of steps down into an underground bunker. The walls had shelves fitted, and there was even an air vent up to the surface.

The man duly left before Rory found a bed which had been made up. The house looked as though it was in use and Rory presumed the occupants were told to go away for the duration of his stay. He worked hard and had completed the circuits just before night fall. He followed the instructions and put the filled boxes down into the bunker on one of the shelves. He saw other boxes there but refrained from looking inside.

He had just finished destroying his instructions when a man entered the kitchen, he was clearly agitated.

'Come on, we had better get away now, I think I was followed. They got held up by a tractor, and some cows coming home, so I think I shook them off. But they may wait for me, there are only so many ways out of here.'

The car drove fast along the narrow roads without lights and Rory was feeling quite sick, when it came to a halt suddenly.

'Christ it's a roadblock,' the man yelled. 'Get out and run, into the woods, go through, keep in the ditch, and hide out in the sheep hut at the end, I'll try and take them away.'

Rory was pushed out as the car reversed madly back up the lane, he ran into the copse just as another car drove down the lane its lights full on. This car drove straight at the reversing car, which swerved off the road, and into a field driving away from the direction Rory was headed. He concentrated on keeping low in the dark, and eventually found the small hut, and hid himself inside.

In the distance he heard gunfire, and the frantic revving of car engines, and then, everything went quiet. Rory stayed hidden in the little hut all the next day, until just before nightfall, when he started to walk away over undulating grassland. In the distance he had seen revolving lights, which he took to be a lighthouse. He followed the light, and eventually came across a road which led into the small fishing town of Balbriggan. In the main street he found a phone box, called Uncle Sean, and told him of his predicament, where he was, and asked if he knew what had happened to his driver, and how he could get help to get back home.

Sean knew Balbriggan and had a friend who, he said, would contact him. He told Rory to go to a pub down the high street. The pub he described was a low white cottage with a stand for milk churns outside. Inside the bar it was dark, with a warm cosy glow emanating from an open fire. The walls were covered with old farming implements, and there were a few alcoves with tables. Rory sat at one of these, so he could see the door, but remain partly hidden. He bought a glass of stout, and had only been there a few minutes, when a man dressed as if he had just stepped off a trawler, entered and sat in the chair opposite.

'Rory, I'm a friend of your Uncle Sean. We've discussed your plight, and we recommend that you take a little sea voyage with me. The Guards are looking for your friend in the car, he smashed his way out, and wrecked a police car, he managed to drive a few miles away, where he abandoned the car. From what I heard, they are only looking for one man, but we can't take chances.'

'Thanks so much, but where will I be going; you say it will be by sea?' asked Rory.

'To some friends of mine, they are in the same sort of struggle as us, and we help each other out on a regular basis, you will be safe with them, at least till the heat dies down. I think you'll like them, they are simple fishing folk like us, good-hearted people.'

Rory's rescuer introduced himself as Fergal, he looked middle aged with grey straggly hair, but had a powerful stocky frame and weathered face. They walked to a small house near the harbour, where Rory was given a huge blue sweater and some oilskin trousers, so that he looked the part. He was also given some US dollars, which Fergal said was an emergency fund.

'You won't need to pay for the trip or lodgings, but they will make you work, this is for expenses, and to get you out of trouble in an emergency you understand.'

They carried some empty crates, which smelt of fish, down to the quay where a wide promenade wound round to a stubby, squat lighthouse. On the rough walls were painted a full range of slogans, interspersed with Irish tri-colours. They walked along to a sizeable black trawler, with a white bridge, the small, curved foredeck was white and there were two large derricks rising skywards, with rigging falling from them ending in massive blocks. To Rory the vessel looked huge, but it was a standard sized trawler capable of going to sea. He carried the crates down onto the deck, and was showed to a small cabin with bunks round the side, and was told that was where he would sleep.

Fergal was the skipper of the trawler, and he explained they often went off the coast of northern Spain to fish, and sometimes even went ashore at small fishing villages, in what was known as the Basque country. However, most of the time, if they had what he called sensitive cargos, they exchanged these at sea, so it would be a trawler from the home port that landed the cargo, along with the catch of fish, if they were lucky.

'We were going to take some of the boxes from the farm

tomorrow, but of course the ones we were getting, were in that car, and we don't know where they ended up. I understand you made them. So what the bosses have said to me now, is, take the boy over to Spain. He can explain what happened, and then he can make some more there. So, it looks as though, you will spend a while in Spain,' said Fergal.

'Do they know what line of work I am in? What I am involved in? Won't it be risky for them to hide me, and will they know what I would need, to make the boxes. Do you know, if they can get the parts I will need?' asked a clearly agitated Rory.

'Oh, they will have an idea, they have been fighting a similar war to us, for some time now. Rory, they are very shrewd operators, trust me. I understand some of the technology they have, is certainly as good as ours. I can imagine that you will earn your keep, they will know by now, what sort of lad you are, and will treat you with respect,' said Fergal, placing a large hand reassuringly on Rory's shoulder.

'Ok, that's good to know, but do they speak English?'

'Not much, but there is a real pretty girl there, who does, but be careful she is fiery, feisty and a passionate Basque,' and Fergal laughed. 'Rory you will be safe with those people, they are good folk. They understand, trust me.'

The sea was a little rough, but Rory managed not to be sick. It took several hours, and after a short sleep he went up and stood on the bridge. He had not been there long before they spotted another trawler in the distance. The two boats signalled to each other by light, and then drew closer together.

There was a long swell, but it was not that rough, so a dinghy was lowered, and Rory together with some boxes was put into it. They pulled alongside the Spanish trawler, which was of similar size as the Balbriggan boat. Rory handed the boxes up, and then was dragged onto the deck of the Spanish vessel by a huge, bearded man who hugged him like a bear. As soon as his feet touched the deck, the man smiled and yelled at him.

'Hola, you're safe now, I am Carlos,' and pointing to a thin lad along the deck, 'he is Pepe. We put your clothes and things below,' he said as he grabbed Rory's bundle of clothes and threw them through an open hatch to the deck beneath. 'That's where you will sleep now, you're going to Spain. Now, we get some more fish, before we get home in morning, ok, you best sleep.'

'Ok, thanks Carlos, just tell me what you want me to do, and I'll do it,' yelled Rory, his voice lost in the wind.

Carlos just pointed below and smiled.

'You're safe now, no worries, you sleep, we fish. It's hard work and dangerous for you on deck, as you are not used to it.'

Rory did as they asked him and went below. The trawler did not seem to roll as much as the Irish one, and all he felt was the throb of the engines, and the occasional sound of machinery being used to haul nets up and onto the deck, the rhythm of the sea eased him into a slumber.

He had no idea of the time when Pepe woke him, but the sun was just clearing the horizon, and there were green hills behind the shoreline, and what looked like mountains in the distance. The rear of the trawler was followed by a crowd of squawking gulls, diving around each other in a bizarre ballet, skimming off the surface of the waves. They moved ever closer to the hills. Pepe grinned a toothy grin and handed him a bread roll, filled with a form of sausage meat, which tasted good, and some strong sweet coffee.

The trawler pulled in past a breakwater, and into a small harbour tying up alongside. Behind the harbours quayside was a row of white buildings topped with red tiled roofs. A couple of shops and bars formed the quayside frontage, with houses going back into the hillside, either side of narrow streets. At one end of the village, there were buildings associated with the care of the few trawlers that hugged the quay, showing that this was a working village not yet consumed by tourism. One shed with double doors wide open had plastic trays stacked outside with a few lobster pots and a mass of multi coloured nets in a heap. Just to the side stood a short stocky woman and a tall slim girl. A brief exchange occurred between Carlos and the older woman in Spanish, with both parties waving their arms vigorously.

'Senora mad, so little fish, and one, just one big one, you, and you don't look that good to eat she say,' chuckled Carlos.

The girl looked for all the world like a flamenco dancer and stared at Rory with dark eyes, she shook her head, and in perfect English said, 'so you are the catch of the day, so do tell me, to what do we owe this honour?'

'I am in a little trouble back in Ireland, and I need shelter, and I believe you have offered me sanctuary,' said Rory.

'I worked that out for myself, how long do you think you will stay, and how will you pay?' was her sharp reply.

'I believe, I have some work to do here, and that is the form of payment, I was told to offer. Your English is very good,' said Rory.

'And you have no Spanish, you people are so lazy. I went to London and studied history and politics, and learnt English as I studied, and now I cook and serve fish, fish which I don't see many of tonight.'

Carlos had been engaged in a heated discussion with the older lady, who transpired to be his wife. He grabbed Rory's belongings and beckoned him to follow. They went to a little restaurant, situated on the quayside. There was a menu of Spanish cuisine based around fish, game, and chicken, itemised on a billboard just outside on the pavement.

'It will be ok, first we eat, then we sleep, tomorrow we talk,' said Carlos.

Carlos's wife was called Delores, and she brushed past her husband and went to a small back room, where she started to make up a bed. As she passed Rory she smiled in a kindly fashion, patted him on the arm and drew him into the room. She spoke softly in Spanish and pointed to a small chest of drawers, in dark wood, across the room from the bed.

'Clothes,' she said, and smiled.

Above the bed was a picture of Christ, illuminated by the rays of the Sun. A small window was covered with floral curtains and outside there were wooden shutters, painted blue, which hid the interior of the room from the world outside. There was a small bedside cupboard, with a light on it, next to the bed. Rory unpacked his notes first, and slid them into the drawer, where a Bible lurked at the back. He unpacked the only clothes he had, which consisted of all he stood in, when he left the farm in Eire and what Fergal had kitted him out with before he embarked on the trawler.

He had entered the restaurant from the kitchen and retraced his steps, and there he found the girl stirring a pot of rabbit stew. She said her name was Maria, and sighed looking at him, with dark almost threatening eyes.

'So, you are Rory, on the run, a Provisional IRA man, a fugitive,' she said.

'I guess that about sums it up,' he replied.

'You have been to university too I understand, studying what?'

'Electronic engineering,' said Rory.

'Ah now, it all starts to make sense, so you will work for us?'

'I believe so,' he replied.

'You are in the Basque homeland; we are passionate people striving for our independence. Do you know what that means?' She said as she moved close to him, and fixed him with cold dark eyes.

'I think so, I was in a similar place, and under similar circumstances to you. In Ireland we are looking for unity, because our island is split apart by history.'

'Well soon you will know where you are, and rest assured we don't suffer fools gladly. You must realise, you could spell trouble for us, just by being here,' she said quietly.

Carlos entered the kitchen and said, 'Maria, be gentle with Rory, he is our guest.'

'He will have to earn our trust and respect,' she said in English and then added more in Spanish, delivered with passion.

Carlos replied in Spanish and added, 'Rory is a good boy, he too has suffered much Maria, what he brings will help our cause, he is an engineer with knowledge we don't have here.'

'The work you were sent here to do, can't be done in the open, so you will have to work in the restaurant too, you understand, it will be your cover, and you will have to learn Spanish fast,' she said.

'I would like to do that anyway Maria, I am so grateful, for all that has been done for me, and I am in your debt. I promise you I will repay that debt, in full.'

'Mmmmm, we will see,' and she swung away from him, with a swish of her skirt.

They ate the rabbit stew and drank some wine, and Rory was quizzed by Maria as to his home life, and what had driven him into the IRA. Delores was given a translation by Carlos, and she gave Rory a hug, before he retired for the night to his little room.

The morning sun shone straight through the cracks in the shutters to herald the new dawn. Rory opened the shutters a little way, and looked out onto a small square, with a tree in its centre. Across the road was a bench against a whitewashed wall. On the bench sat three old men looking out across the harbour, through the gap that formed the narrow street running down the side of the restaurant. He was suddenly aware of a presence behind him, it was Maria looking over his shoulder to the scene beneath.

'I don't want my family put at risk again. I have already lost someone dear to me, killed by the Guardia Civil, I did not mention that last night, as it is still very painful to talk about. So, you will do as I say at all times, or you will never see Ireland again, is that clear.'

'Crystal clear, as you know, I too lost someone dear to me, and she had nothing to do with the struggles, and the politics, we were caught up in. I do not know yet, what you want from me, but I will do all I can to repay your hospitality. Maria, I am a simple man, and what you see is what you get, I have no hidden agenda. I am here because my Uncle Sean, and his friend, the fisherman Fergal said I would be safe with Carlos and his family in Spain, that is, until the situation changes. I don't know when that will be, I am just waiting for instructions from my Uncle Sean or Carlos.' She looked at him intently, so that he felt uncomfortable, but he met her stare.

'You will play the part of a friend from university in England, you are here to study Spanish, and Spanish, or rather Basque culture. To earn your way, and your keep here in the restaurant, you will work as a waiter. You will not do anything stupid, and for the start keep yourself to yourself, is that clear. I will be watching you, do not get the impression I am a soft touch, I have done things for my cause, that any girl should not be expected to do. I'll put some books about our homeland in your room, read them, two are in English.'

'Thank you, I will read them; I appreciate the trouble you are taking,' he said.

'Right, now come, you will set the tables for lunch.'

The little restaurant had a dark interior with tables running down one side of the main room, each table was separated by a screen of wood, giving the diners privacy. The tables each seated six people and opposite this row of alcoves was a bar stocked with local wines and spirits, and a machine for dispensing coffee. Down from the bar, was the door to the kitchen, and one leading to a toilet. Outside on the pavement there were a few more tables.

Lunchtime is a protracted affair in Spain, as Rory was about to find out, and he soon got the hang of the menu. The customers that day were all local people, so Rory had time to get to know the menu, and the common phrases they used. Maria introduced him as her friend from England there to learn about the Basque region and its culture. A couple of older men nodded, and it was obvious from Maria's response, they knew he was there for other reasons than a study of their culture. Everyone who came in that lunchtime gave him a warm welcome, and he began to relax.

Rory fitted in well with the family schedule, he found that Carlos was just a gentle giant and Delores started to treat him like the son she never had. Maria was more guarded but even she smiled now and again, however, she played the role of his friend from university to perfection, in public. His education in the Spanish language was conducted by the whole family and several of the locals. Maria gave him some books in Spanish, and she spent time educating him in the written word. They found that he was a willing student, who was not afraid of hard work and a quick learner.

He went out on Carlos's trawler for several trips, and formed a real friendship with Pepe, who gave the impression that he was a little crazy, but he always did the right thing at the right time. He was a good sailor and showed Rory how to mend nets and splice rope. The work on the trawler was hard physical work, and Pepe for all his skinny appearance, was immensely strong.

In a quiet moment Rory said to Maria, 'I hope my Spanish is improving, the locals seem to understand me, and they give me the impression they like me, as much as I like them.'

'Don't be fooled, it'll take more than a few games of chess, and a few beers, to gain their trust, as they have been let done so many times before, but once gained, you'll not find any truer friends, and someday, you may need that friendship. Rory, they do say they like you, and that is a good start.'

'Maria, it's a good life here, and I wish in many respects, that it does not end. I am so grateful for the welcome, but I feel I should be paying you back, where do I go from here?'

'Be patient Rory, you will know, soon enough. When the need arises, you will be contacted.' She said and patted him lightly on the hand. Over the days her stare had softened, and she liked the way he had embraced the Basque way of life.

A few days later, one of the old men who used to sit on

the bench opposite his window, came into the restaurant early in the morning as Rory was cleaning the floor.

'Rory, come sit with me, Maria will make us a coffee. Your Spanish is getting really good now, you have worked hard at it, and you, soon, will speak better than me.' He chuckled. 'I have a friend who would like to talk to you.'

'That's fine just say where and when,' said Rory.

'We will take a trip, up into the hills this morning, to meet him.'

'Ok, but I will have to tell Delores,' said Rory.

'That's all-right Maria knows where you are going, and so does Delores.' Maria leant over the counter, and nodded.

The man took him to a battered old Seat, and they clattered over the old road out of the village, up onward to the foothills of the Pyrenees. The old car spluttered up along steep sided roads, lined with beech trees, at about five hundred metres high, the trees suddenly changed to birch and oak and at over a thousand metres they became chestnut. A large bird of prey flew alongside them for a while and the old man said it was a golden eagle. On a rocky ledge they saw some wild goats standing erect looking down onto the road.

The old man's name was Pablo, he was a gentle, kindly old man, who had spoken to Rory in the restaurant a few times, but now they chatted freely. Rory gave him a potted history of his life, and the problems in Ireland. Pablo responded telling him more of the history of the Basque struggle for independence, and it became very apparent that Pablo was a passionate Basque.

As they neared a remote village, tucked in amidst pointed rocks, Pablo told Rory he was going to meet a man, who was interested in his skills as an engineer and wanted to establish, if he could help them with a particular project, the details of which he was not party to. They parked in a small square at the centre of the village, and Pablo lead Rory down a narrow little alley, to a small café.

There was a narrow entrance, with a bar to the left-hand side of a long corridor, a coffee machine sat on a shelf on the rear wall. The counter had a glass display with a few cakes in it, a couple of tables sat against the wall to the right. Steps at the end of the corridor lead down to the main area, where there were few tables, this area was poorly lit, the gloom made worse by the fact that they had entered from the bright morning sunlight.

A man in his fifties with a swarthy complexion, and a full head of black curly hair, which made him look more like an Andalusian gypsy than a Basque, sat at a table watching Rory enter. He smiled and indicated to Rory to sit. Pablo had gone back to the entrance to order himself a coffee and some cake from a thin woman, with pinched face, who suddenly appeared at the bar. She came down the steps with a tray of coffee and some crescent shaped pastries.

The man spoke in Spanish 'I understand Maria has been teaching you Spanish, she says that you are a good pupil, few people who come to our country make the effort, which is sad.'

'Maria is a good teacher,' said Rory.

'She likes you, and these days she finds it hard to like

62

anyone she does not know, she has gone through much, as it appears, so have you. How is my good friend Sean these days, still drinking bad whisky no doubt?'

Rory chuckled 'you obviously know Uncle Sean.'

'Oh, yes we have met, he speaks well of you Rory.'

'I never knew he had friends in Spain.'

'No, nor should you, that is how we stay safe.'

The man gave his name as Pedro and he went on to briefly outline that the Basques and the Irish had a good deal of history together over centuries, and that they had supported each other when times were hard.

Rory said that he had been brought up in a Republican house, and had known nothing, but what was known as the 'troubles' and the heartache they brought, without elaborating.

Pedro said he had just wanted to see and speak with Rory, face to face. He said he liked what he saw, and that Rory was level-headed, which was essential.

'We've been having problems in certain areas and wish to rectify them. I have projects in mind, that need technical solutions, and I understand you have the expertise, to solve those problems,' explained Pedro.

'Without knowing what they are, I will not know for sure if I can solve them. I presume these involve electronics, because that is what I studied at university,' said Rory.

'They are similar devices to the ones you were working on, so I will need to know what items you will require, to make them, and what tools you will need.'

'I have notes hidden, back at the restaurant, and these can be used to form a list. It would be a good idea not to have a single person buying all of the component parts, of course.'

'I understand, and are your notes well hidden?' asked Pedro.

'Yes' said Rory.

'Can you commit the list to memory?'

'For the most part yes, for the major components, like integrated circuits, but I will need many more common components, such as resistors and capacitors, and these I could not possibly memorise,' explained Rory. 'The common components, if seen on a list, would not arise any suspicion. It is only the major integrated circuits used in timing, and coding, that would lead someone, to work out what the end product was. Have you anyone in the trade, that could buy the common components without raising any comment?'

'Oh yes, we have friends in that trade, they repair radios and communication equipment, I assume they will know,' said Pedro nodding.

'They will, and I can ask them to get the more complex items, possible by mail order, a few at a time, as a big order of some of these, would immediately ring alarm bells.'

'That's good Rory. Please keep your council, and do not discuss what I have asked for, with anyone, except possibly, Maria. Walls have ears, I think is the phrase, you use. Write a list for me, put it in a sealed container and give it to Pablo, put on the list any tools you will need. We will have them here for you to work on safely up in the mountains, away from prying eyes. You will take a short holiday with Maria, amidst our lovely mountain scenery, in our mountain air, and with a pretty girl, what more could a man want,' he chuckled. 'Maria will be your security, she is good, and you can trust her.'

Rory nodded.

'Now my friend, another coffee? Pablo, join us,' said Pedro waving his hand towards the bar.

Pablo, followed by the lady carrying another tray of coffee, came down the stairs, and sat with them.

'Pablo, look after my young friend here. Rory, Pablo sees everything in the village, he will give a warning of any trouble .'

'Of course, Pedro, he is a good boy, I will look after him,' said a smiling Pablo.

They sat for a few minutes more talking about the politics of their respective situations, before Rory and Pablo left to drive down the mountain.

At the restaurant Maria grabs Rory as he enters the door.

'Come darling, where have you been, we have lunch to prepare, important customers?'

She drags him into the kitchen.

'Something is wrong Maria?' he says seeing the fierce darting eyes.

'Yes, Rory there is a man inside, at the table near the door, he is dangerous. We know he is an informant; he is also a drug dealer who will do anything to make money. He has some of the local Police in his pocket, say as little as possible and only in Spanish. Collect the plates at the table opposite, look at him, not too obviously. Then come back to the kitchen.'

A squat man with black hair, his nose hooked, fleshy lips

and small eyes was the caricature of an evil pantomime villain. He looked up as Rory collected the plates and his eyes narrowed. Rory immediately got the impression he would be manipulative and devious. There were two other men with him, they had their back to him, but it was so obvious that this was the man Maria was talking about. Rory went quickly back into the kitchen.

Carlos had come into the bar. The man waved towards Rory.

'Carlos, you are taking on more staff I see, or is he another lover for Maria?'

'Why would I want a lover, with so many admirers such as you,' Maria said in a toneless voice. 'More wine, Senor?'

'Who is he?' asked the voice, in a mocking tone.

'Just another boy. working through college, he is learning Spanish. He has no money, so he has to work.'

Rory had stood next to the kitchen door listening, Delores was standing behind him.

'Bastard, say nothing to him, he is evil, he and his friends they try to get Carlos to move drugs for them, he gets people to take risks for him, or he makes trouble for them if they refuse,' whispered Delores.

Maria opened the kitchen door and yelled in 'Senor Rodriguez is waiting for his paella.'

'You will serve us, Maria?' he asked.

'Of course Senor, but if you touch me, I will stab you,' she said in a mocking tone.

'She is feisty today, or maybe, it is the wrong phase of the moon,' was his reply.

'Always Senor,' she countered.

'Five minutes,' yelled Delores through the door.

She then filled a large metal pan with the paella and collected large deep plates, before walking out and dumping it on the table. The men sat for most of the afternoon drinking brandy before they left. They called Carlos to the table to drink with them, but he made his excuses and went back to his boat. Maria waited on them, and never left the bar area.

When they left she came into the kitchen to Rory.

'I told them you were studying Spanish culture, art, and also learning the language. Have you your papers, and are they in order?' she said anxiously.

'Yes, my uncle sent them to me in the post, passport, Student Union Card, and some medical insurance papers, everything he could think of,' said Rory.

'That is good that you have your papers, keep them safe, he could send someone, Police, to check, he will want to know who you are, knowing him.'

Carlos returned after the men left.

'I had meant to ask you about your papers, it is good Rory you have them. You could be here for a while, and that man, will make trouble if he can. He is always looking for a lever, to use me, to get me to do things for him, and always for free. He will blackmail me, if he can, he is so devious, he cares only for money. He is not a true Basque. You must be careful, say nothing to him,' warned Carlos.

'Is he that bad?' asked Rory.

'Oh, yes, he is rich and lives his life of crime, for fun, he takes a delight in causing pain. I am sure as a child, he would pull the wings off butterflies. The café always empties when he comes in,' added Maria.

'How did your trip to the mountains go' asked Carlos.

'Good I think, I met Pedro, and he said I would be back to the mountains, with Maria, to look at nature and the beautiful scenery. That is, when they have the supplies and tools I need. He said you would protect me Maria?' Rory chuckled.

'Oh, lucky me,' said Maria with a smile, and she blew him a kiss.

Carlos chuckled 'we don't need to know the details, it's safer that way, especially with Rodriguez sniffing around. I know he has a consignment to move down the coast, and no boat will take him. He will use any excuse to divert the Guardia's attention, so we must be careful.'

'So, I had better learn something about Spanish art, apart from Picasso, Velazquez and Goya,' said Rory.

'I am impressed,' said Maria.

'Apart from Guernica, I know nothing of art from this region.'

'Art in our homeland goes back fifteen thousand years, to the cave paintings at Altamira and Pozalagua, so you have much to see, and some local artists, Juan Zurikoudae, Roman and Valentin Zublauvre, it is a shame that your study is not for real, but I can lend you some books, and it will do your Spanish some good too.'

'I would like that,' said Rory quite genuinely.

Two weeks passed; Rodriguez made a couple more visits to Carlos, who still refused to ship any of his 'merchandise.' On one occasion he saw Rory, and fortunately Rory was reading a book on Goya.

'So you are an art student, looking at his romantic period I see.'

Rory did not look up and replied simply 'yes.'

Maria appeared, from nowhere.

'And what do you want now?' she demanded.

'Is Carlos here?' he asked impatiently.

'No' replied Maria, 'he has better things to do than see you.'

'Oh really, I wonder what it is that keeps him so busy, that he can't help an old friend anymore?'

'I will tell him you called' she said clearing tables, 'now, is there anything else.'

'A brandy, for your greatest admirer possibly,' he said with a grin.

She poured him a brandy and slid it along the bar counter.

'There, service with a smile.' But there was no smile from Maria.

Rory kept reading and then wrote something in a notebook, watched over by Rodriguez with interest. He gulped down the brandy and without paying left.

'That was good Rory, he still suspects something is going on, but he does not know what, he cannot understand, why the locals have taken to you so readily, I think that worries him. Seeing you with the art books, was good cover. Actually, I like to draw Rory, I am no good, but it relaxes me,' she said.

'I think you are good, I have seen some of your sketches, Delores showed me,' said Rory.

'Thank you, Rory that means a lot,' she said with a smile,

and touched his hand as a mark of genuine affection, rarely shown since her boyfriend had been taken from her.

Two days later Maria woke Rory early.

'We go now,' she said.

They went in Carlos's old van, heading east towards France, and then turned inland, and climbed up into the Pyrenees. The soil turned to a reddish pink, and then, they were in a forested region ,where the roads became much narrower and steeper. Overhead a golden eagle floated on the wind, as on the journey he had with Pablo. They rounded a sharp corner where a small chapel, housing a picture of the 'Virgin Mary,' stood overlooking a steep sided gorge, where a river ran swiftly over rocks, in a white-water torrent. A young man dressed in jeans and a check shirt stood on what was a viewing point for the scene below. Maria swung the van in beside him.

'Hello Maria, and I take it this is Rory, hello I am Luis, I have heard everything about you.' He smiled and embraced Maria before giving him a hug too. 'Right, I will drive from here, Maria.'

'God have mercy on us then' she said, 'I want to live to an old age, so don't go mad.' He laughed and swung the old van off the platform, and at breakneck speed went down the road, with no regard for any possible oncoming traffic, before turning off in a cloud of dust, along a narrow track causing the van to leap at every hole in the path and bump and jump precariously. On they went into a dense forest before pulling up at a wooden 'foresters hut.'

The building was surprisingly spacious inside, it consisted of a single room split into areas for cooking and for sleeping. There were no beds, just low benches. Cooking appeared to be done on a log burning stove, and there was a chemical toilet outside in a separate hut.

'Since you were here last Maria, we have had electricity run in, so our friend can operate, do not try to rig up a light, as it may attract attention, just use the candles as before, Maria. The people at the farm will bring you food, and also keep watch.'

'It's so quiet here, I am sure we could hear anyone coming for miles,' observed Rory.

'The Guardia use horses, and are very quiet, and please don't wander looking at nature, as you could easily get lost Rory,' warned Luis.

'Ok, I am sure Maria will keep me under control.'

'There is an old empty water tank over there between the trees, hidden by the bank, and covered with moss and lichen, it acts as a sort of dead letter box, and that is where you will find all the stuff you will need. Tomorrow, Jose will check to see you have everything. Now, have a good evening, there is cold food and a bottle of wine, in the kitchen cupboard.' With that he left on foot, and vanished through the trees that screened the farm.

Rory had a quick look at the contents of the bunker, which appeared to be all the things on the list he had asked for.

In the cabin within another cupboard, they found sleeping bags and blankets. They were like an old couple on holiday sitting at the table with their fresh bread and cold meat, each with a glass of red wine. After the meal they sat on the balcony outside, looking up through the treetops at the moonlight and a canopy of stars.

Maria was first up in the morning, just as the sun tried to force its way through the trees. The colours of the sunrise made small glades of light in the openings between the trees. She made a breakfast of cheese and bread washed down with fresh orange juice. Rory slept through all her preparations, and she had to wake him.

They had just finished eating when Pedro appeared, without making a sound, with him was a tall young man with glasses, who he introduced as Jose. He said that it was Jose, who had coordinated the acquisition of all the equipment.

'Jose will stay with you, and help make the devices I require,' said Pedro. 'I want thirty timers, ten short delay, of four hours, the rest will be for ten, twenty and thirty days, ten of each. Once these have been done, I would like you to devise five sequential firing units, for our rockets. The rockets are initiated, by a simple electronic firing system. The launcher will fire five rockets, one after the other, with a short delay between each firing. Please do what you can, and you will have our gratitude. Is that ok?'

'Yes, everything looks good, it appears I have what I need, and I will be glad of some skilled help, especially from someone involved with your current systems,' said Rory.

'I would love to stay, but I know you will be safe with Maria, as you probably have seen, there are firearms in the bunker. I will have people in the woods too, you won't see them, but if you hear a shot fired, that is a danger signal, and you will do whatever Maria tells you, is that clear.'

'Yes,' they said in unison.

Pedro dropped his large satchel on the floor.

'That is lunch, 'bon appetite,' the people at the farm are friends Rory, you can trust them. When you have finished, Maria will get a message to me.'

Pedro left as silently and quickly as he had appeared.

Jose it transpired had studied electronic engineering at university too, and his course had been very similar to Rory's.

'Rory, it was very clever of you to do the artworks for the circuits, and combine them all into one board, and I was glad you had done the patterns. I hated the thought of playing around with Vero board. I got the boards printed, so we have just to cut out the individual circuits, and drill them,' said Jose.

'I had forgotten I had done that; I am so glad, you got them etched, it is going to save a great deal of time,' said Rory.

'A firm local to me, printed the patterns onto photo resist board, they had no idea what they were for, and I told them it was a project for the university. They don't care, as long as they get their money.'

The two lads got on well straight away, and threw themselves into the tasks.

'I'll go for a stroll to the farm, you are watched and will be safe, but if you want me, just whistle. Now play nicely both of you,' said Maria with a smile.

They had soon made a prototype for the timers, and tested it successfully, and quickly established a production line. It was getting dark when they finished the first part of their task, as Maria returned.

'I have some hot food from the farm, Jose you are to stay with us tonight.'

Up to that point they had just discussed the making of the timers, but now they relaxed. Jose said he came from an ancient Basque family and was passionate about Basque independence, but he had definite reservations about the armed struggle. He said his stance was hardened after the Guardia had raided his parent's house, looking for a fugitive, who was not there and they shot his father when he attempted to stop them taking his daughter, whose boyfriend was a suspected ETA member.

'I so want a political solution,' said Jose, 'but they won't listen. It seems all three of us have suffered tragedy, because of politics, in one way or other, mostly because little men, want to appear big, and if you do not go along with their ideas, you will be crushed. Sorry I am rambling, but I do so hate violence.' He said with passion. 'But, I have been sucked into it, and I can't see any alternative.'

'I do so understand Jose, I do wish there was an alternative,' said Rory.

'If enough good men and women stand firm, they will succeed, history shows that,' said Maria with conviction.

'If you believe your cause to be just, I am sure you will succeed, it will just take time, and a great deal of heartache,' said Rory.

'Don't get me wrong, I fully understand, I don't ask you for justification of any violence. What does make me annoyed, is that some of us are taking the risks, for those who will be the ones to benefit, on a personal political level,' said Jose.

'Yes, that's so true,' added Maria.

'All I hope for now, is that this is not a case of '*déjà vu*,' as I was ambushed, when I last made timers for someone' said Rory with a sigh. 'It's not been all bad, because, here I am in Spain with friends.'

'We will be safe there are watchers, who know this forest better than anyone, they will be watching our back,' said Maria. With that reassurance they got tucked into their sleeping bags for the night.

In the morning Pedro came to the hut before sunrise. He looked concerned and immediately told them his impatience got the better of him, and he wanted to know how they were getting on. Jose told him they had made their immediate target, as the timers had been made, ahead of schedule.

'They are all marked up with the delay, and are in the bunker as arranged Pedro,' said Jose.

Pedro said he would take them all, as the planned operation had had to be brought forward. Jose said they had not done any work on the sequential timers yet, and asked if that meant that particular task would be abandoned.

'Those devices are for another group; they are impatient, so is there any chance, you can get them done in a day?' asked Pedro.

'That's a tall order, we don't have any printed circuit boards, we will have to do it all on Vero board,' said Jose.

'We have a deal with them, so please do your best. They want to see you, but I won't let them, they have their own agenda, and it is not always in the best interests of the cause,' said Pedro, with a glance at Maria.

'I don't like the sound of that Pedro, who are these people, as if I didn't know?' she said.

'It'll be alright, just try to get those devices done quickly, put them into the bunker. We will tell them where to collect them tonight.'

'No pressure then,' said Rory.

'How will they know how to operate them; we don't know for sure how to connect them up to the rockets?' said Jose.

'They will have to work that out for themselves. I have no idea how their weapon works either. They have never told me. How long do you estimate it will take?' asked Pedro.

'At least four hours, I am just going to use the same system we devised for sequential fired mortars, back in Ireland,' said Rory. 'But, we won't have any time to test them.'

'That will be ok, do the best you can. Now I have to go.'

'Wait a minute Pedro, who are we dealing with, not the group from Ituren' demanded Maria.

'Yes, sadly,' he replied.

'That shit Rodriguez runs that group, in all but name, you have set us up for a lot of trouble,' added Maria.

'He does not know it is you, who are here, if there is any trouble just get out before he can identify you,' said Pedro. 'I have the area covered we will know, when any of the group are coming anywhere near.'

'He is annoyed with Carlos at the moment, because he won't move his drug shipment down the coast for him. If he finds out it is us doing this, he will cause trouble, you know that,' said Maria.

'The most important thing is for him not to find out it is Rory and Jose, who are the engineers, he wants someone with technical ability for his group, someone he can control, and get to produce weapons as, and when, he needs them. He'll offer them at a price no doubt. It is money, and not the cause, he truly respects. It is most important, that you don't let his group get their hands on Rory or Jose, Maria.'

'Why don't we just leave now,' said Jose.

'It is politics, he'll make capital, if we don't deliver for the cause, he will use any failure to meet requirements, to cause problems for our group, and raise his own profile. He is just looking to increase his own standing in the movement, at our expense, as well as make money on the side, as he can,' said Pedro.

'You have put us between a hammer and an anvil,' said Maria.

Jose banged the table, 'this is not going to help the situation. We have a tight deadline, so we are wasting time, debating issues, we can't resolve.'

'Get something done, please,' said Pedro.

'And if they do not work, because we can't test them. What are they likely to do? We don't have the rocket system, which we would need,' said Jose.

'That will be their problem, they will be told the timers were tested and any problem will be their fault. It's up to them to connect them to their system,' said Pedro with a shrug.

'The circuits sound complicated, but they are actually

simple, so they should work, if connected up properly. But, any failure could result in them trying to find us, and get us to set up the system for them, surely,' said Jose.

'Let me handle that, they are very secretive about how their rockets work, I can't see them sharing that technology with you,' said Pedro. 'There are many who realise what sort of man Rodriguez is, his days are numbered.'

'Which makes him particularly dangerous,' added Maria.

'Let us get going,' urged Jose.

It took just under the four hours for the circuits to be made and packaged.

'Ok, let us put them in the bunker and get out of here, I will bring the van round,' said Maria. 'How will you get home Jose?'

'As quickly as possible, I will walk over the mountain, no one will see me, I know this area better than most, don't worry about me,' said Jose. I feel it is getting a little tense here, so I will go now, if that's ok.'

They hugged and Jose slipped into the trees. As Maria brought the van up to the door of the hut, they heard a gunshot.

'Right, that is a signal, let us go! Now! Rory,' shouted Maria 'get in the van they will be close, I do not want them to see us.'

She accelerated the van as fast as she could and started off down the road, just as two men appeared, on the road behind them. One produced a handgun and fired at the back of the van, missing by a distance.

Maria suddenly swung off the road, into the air, with the

poor old van crashing down on hard ground, and into an olive grove. They sped through the trees, the van's engine screaming in pain, and onto a road at the other side of the grove.

'They have to get to their vehicle, and they won't have expected us to do that, with this poor old van, they don't know who we are, and which way we will be going. So, we have distance on them, but I will have to push this poor old van as fast as it will go.'

As they sped along Rory asked Maria why Rodriguez was acting the way he did.

'Rodriguez and Pedro are in a power struggle to control ETA in this region, Rodriguez wants total power, so he can line his pockets. Pedro wants the political power in a free Basque country.'

The journey took far less time than the outward journey and they were back at the restaurant in record time.

Delores, with Pablo, met them at the restaurant.

'That shit Rodriguez set Carlos up, and the Guardia have arrested him for having drugs on his boat. They have confiscated the trawler too,' said a distraught Pablo.

'They are asking where Maria and the Englishman are,' said Delores 'I have your papers here Rory, you will have to get out of here as quick as you can. Pablo has heard he knows what you are doing here. I told the Guardia you were in Madrid studying art at the Prado. But he is sure you are not, but he could not convince the Guardia, at least while I was there, but that will change I feel sure.'

'Rodriguez is convinced you are with Pedro. It is not safe, you have to go; we have Anton's old car for you,' said Pablo.

Delores hugged them both, 'now go quick to Uncle Luigi he is expecting you.'

They found the car and drove away back into the Pyrenees.

Chapter 3

الزمن لا يتغير، الزمن يكشف.

Time doesn't change, time reveals.

I t was a wet wintry night in North London, an elderly man staggered along the Holloway Road towards the Royal Northern Hospital. He stopped in a shop doorway, and gently collapsed onto the pavement. Police Constable Stuart Gerrard walking along behind him, asked if he was alright, checking to see if he smelt of drink. The man tried to speak, before going limp. Gerrard called for an ambulance. One fortunately was close, and he was lifted inside for the journey, of a few yards, to the hospital where he was pronounced dead on arrival.

The officer with the casualty sister searched his pockets to establish his identity. They found an envelope postmarked from America in his pockets, with diagrams of electronic circuits, one of which looked like an improvised weapons system. All the writings with the diagrams, were in some form of code. The sister agreed with the officer, that they had a sinister aspect to them. There was nothing else on him that gave them any idea of who he was, and thus who the next of kin would be.

Detective Sergeant Forrester was on duty that night in the CID office, at Holloway Police Station and PC Gerrard said to the sister 'I am going to get DS Forrester to look at these papers, its fortunate he is on duty tonight, he came to us from the Anti-Terrorist Branch. I think he should have a look at this man and these letters, can you keep him here for a while.'

'I don't think he will complain, and he isn't going anywhere quickly,' said the sister.

John Forrester had just finished with a prisoner at Hornsey Police Station and joined them twenty minutes later.

'I'm sure you are right, who the hell is he? I am going to take possession of the letters, sister, they need to be looked at by an expert, I am fairly sure we are dealing with some form of terrorist device,' said John Forrester.

The sister was happy, once a signature was obtained on the property form.

'Stuart, I will get this stuff faxed over to Fred Adams at the Bomb Data Centre at the Yard, to see what he thinks of it. Let us make the letters an exhibit, and we will get him fingerprinted now, to see if that will help with identification,' said Forrester.

The pictures elicited an instant response from Fred Adams once he saw them. He phoned John Forrester, just catching him before he went off duty.

'Can you get all his property and put it safe for us? One of the diagrams is the same circuitry, that we saw in the incendiary devices put down in shops in Oxford Street, last Christmas, that were claimed by PIRA,' said Fred. 'I'll be over this morning, as soon as I can get away. Thanks for taking his prints, we can run them through our data bases, and the Irish ones too, it will be interesting to see who he was talking to in the states, as well as finding out, who he is.'

Fred duly attended Holloway Police Station with an Exhibits Officer Paul Wright, John Forrester was waiting for them.

'It's odd, he hardly has any money on him, and no credit cards. The only line of investigation we appear to have, is the hotel key, hopefully there will be something there. Those letters are a real puzzle. Is anyone you know good at code breaking?' Fred chuckled.

'Don't look at me Fred, I am hopeless at crosswords, and this looks like a job for Bletchley Park,' said John Forrester. 'Gerrard found him collapsed in a doorway, in the Holloway Road, last night, he showed no sign of any injury, and the hospital have said he died of a heart attack, but that will have to be confirmed by the PM. The only writing in normal English, is an address in Tottenham Court Road, and what looks like a phone number.'

'I am fairly sure that address, is an electronics shop. So, was he going to get some of the components, which feature in those circuits? We recognise a couple of the circuits, but some are foreign to me,' said Fred Adams. 'The MOD scientists will be fascinated, I am sure. So, I need a photocopy of all of them, to send them to the Fort as soon as possible. The DI who is dealing with the incendiary devices is a good man, and he is already interested, and has squared this with your DI. Oh, and please thank PC Gerrard for me, he obviously used his head.'

'He is a good lad I will let him know, he will appreciate that,' said John Forrester with a smile.

A logo on the hotel key led to them identifying it as the 'Grange' in Wood Green. A search of the man's room revealed a small case with a change of clothes, but no form of identification. The name given to the hotel reception was John Smith, and he had paid in advance, for three days, in cash.

At the electronics shop in Tottenham Court Road an assistant remembered the man, who spoke with a soft Irish voice. He asked for specific integrated circuits and paid cash. The circuits included timing and decoding circuits. The shop was busy at the time, and the assistant did not think twice about the purchase.

The electronics expert at the MOD laboratory confirmed that some of the circuits were circuits used in the incendiary devices planted by PIRA, the previous Christmas. He said that at first glance the other circuits could well be for timers, remote control devices and a variety of booby trap and anti-handling devices, but, he would have to study them further to see what the man was planning.

'The author certainly knows what he is about, and if they start making, and using this lot, we could be in for a torrid time, or, rather your colleagues on the street will,' was the comment from the scientist.

The number on the envelope turned out, not to be a telephone number, but that of an integrated timer circuit, which would make the construction of any timed circuit, a lot simpler, and more reliable than those currently used by the PIRA. The IC was made by a company in the USA, who had a subsidiary company in London. A search of the recent sales of the item showed a considerable number had been purchased by an electronics shop in Manchester. The shop there had put in the order for an Irishman, who placed the order at the counter, and paid cash in advance, asking the shop to order them for him. The name and address he gave in Eire was false, however, he provided a phone number in Manchester where he could be contacted once the goods arrived at the shop.

The address for the phone was visited, and a man was arrested and taken to the local Police station. He was identified as a local thief, but had no previous connections to PIRA.

At first, he denied knowledge of the purchase, until a receipt was found for the goods. He then, said, that he had been approached by 'a man in the pub' who had persuaded him to make the purchase on his behalf, and he would be paid for doing it. He said that they looked to be innocent items and the man had told him they were for mending TVs, and were hard to get and would be subject to a heavy import tax. He thought it would be 'money for old rope' and was happy to go along with it especially as he had been given the cash needed in advance. The man had told him to post them for him to an address in Eire. At first he said he had forgotten the address but the Detectives found an

Irish address on a note pad, and the man admitted that was the address he had sent the components to. The intended recipient was O'Sullivan, at the Old Farmhouse, Kilcaddeary.

The arrested man did not supply any details of the man in the pub, who had originally approached him. He provided a description, which no one believed, was a valid one.

The enquiry was quickly passed to the Ballistics Section of the Garda Siochana in Dublin. Pat Casey was a little puzzled as the address, which was out in the back of beyond, but it rang a faint bell. He said he would look into it himself. It was only a few minutes later, before he was back on the phone.

'This address is a farm, and it was the centre of a recent incident. A suspect in a murder in Dublin was followed to the farm, a roadblock was set up, and two men were seen to leave the farm, get into a car which subsequently crashed the roadblock. The driver, a known PIRA man, was then involved in a shoot-out and died later in hospital, a Guard was injured too. The passenger was never found. No one was found at the farm and there was nothing of interest there either. A local informant said they were mending radios there, but this could not be confirmed. In view of what you say our boys will go back and have another look, we will do a full forensic examination of the place,' said Pat Casey.

'I really appreciate that Pat. Do you know who the passenger was?' asked Fred.

'No, but he was a young man, and managed to disappear

at speed, and vanish,' replied Pat.

The scientists looking at the circuit drawings produced some disturbing theories with respect to the potential weapon systems PIRA could be working on. They were desperate to break the code and got specialists involved. It took them several weeks and still there was no interpretation. The experts all agreed the author was someone who was an expert, with imagination. The drawings were passed on to the FBI for their opinion, but they were not prepared to speculate, at least not to the Anti- terrorist Branch.

A few days later Pat got back in touch with Fred.

'In the farm, we found off cuts of wire, some screwed up tape, and solder blobs, obvious signs they were making up circuits. We found out what some of them were. Under the pigsty we found a metal lined bunker, and inside there were made up electronic circuits. We have fingerprints from the farm, and are processing the made-up timers now. There were a number of electronic components, and the equipment, they used in the production of the circuits. We hope, we can get prints from them too. The integrated circuits that were purchased through Manchester, are here too.'

'How did components, used in the construction of the devices, get to the farmhouse? Do you have any ideas, as to who is transporting the stuff, Pat, and where the equipment came from?' asked Fred.

'No, but someone, must have been going there on a regular basis, not all the stuff came by post that is clear,' said Pat.

One of the team at the Anti-Terrorist Branch was

playing with the codes and almost by accident, isolated the key numbers at the top of each page, and realised they were the numbers of verses from the bible. He then, took a look at the book of numbers, and found the code was based on the text. Once the code was identified the letters were quickly deciphered, and as everyone thought they were letters showing how to make the circuits, and apply them to a range of improvised weapons systems.

The letters in the bunker showed the development of circuits seen in IRA devices already deployed in Ireland. One letter mentioned 'the college in Boston,' and this was passed to the FBI more in hope than anger, however, they came back directly. They identified the author as a Professor John O'Rourke, a professor in electronics based in Boston.

He had been arrested a few years previous for an assault on a colleague and for criminal damage. He had an Irish ancestry, and like so many Irish Americans had romanticised the 'Struggle' in Ireland. When interviewed he said he did not know who the people, he was writing too were. They wanted him to put it into code so that if the letters went astray no one would get into trouble. He kept saying that it was just an academic exercise, and the devices invented were not intended to be put into use. It was just an adventure for him. He claimed he had been approached by a colleague, John Callaghan, who was a structural engineer and a patriotic Irishman. Callaghan had told him, that he was writing a paper on the history and development of terrorist weaponry, as part of a wider study of the 'struggles' in Ireland for the Fenian Society.

Fred sent a photo of the old man who died in London to the FBI, and the professor identified him as John Callaghan. The university in Boston said that he had come there on an academic exchange. He had told the university he had come from the NIHE in Dublin, but they had no record of him, and his true identity remained a mystery, so the trail went cold.

When Pat phoned again it was to confirm what was suspected that the fingerprints on the devices in the bunker were the old man's and some unidentified prints. The letters also had prints belonging to the American professor.

A few days later a man came back to the bunker and was promptly grabbed by the Garda. His fingerprints did not match the unidentified ones and he transpired to be a petty criminal, who immediately wished to distance himself from any PIRA activity. He said he had been paid well in cash, just to collect whatever was in the bunker, and take the items to a warehouse in Navan, he said he had no idea what the items would be.

The man who paid him gave his name as Paddy Malone. The warehouse was owned by a man who had died five years previous and had remained empty ever since. The man had no known relative. The council had started proceedings to get ownership, with a view to demolishing it, as it had become a centre for all sorts of unlawful activities.

The RUC and the Garda drew up a brief list of suspects who had a background in electronic engineering, and had connections to PIRA, but were able to eliminate most of them.

Later that summer the Spanish Police sent details of a

series of incendiary attacks on tourist targets, bars, and restaurants along the Costa del Sol. One of the devices failed and the electronic timer was recovered intact. The circuit was similar to those found in the bunker at the farm in Eire, and used the same integrated circuit at its heart.

The Spanish Police sent an enquiry to the American company but there were no recorded sales in Spain. The forensic team of the Guardia Civil recovered a partial fingerprint from the actual chip on the circuit, within the sealed timer. There was not enough for a criminal prosecution but it matched the prints on the devices found in the Irish cache.

All the records of Irishmen who entered Spain were checked against known IRA suspects, and there were a number of arrests, but they were all later released. The bombings had been claimed in the name of ETA. No one was killed or injured in any of the attacks, and damage to property was minimal, but the damage to tourism was immense.

As a known ETA, and criminal mastermind, suspicion fell on Rodriguez who immediately tried to deflect suspicion onto Carlos and the Englishman staying with him. Carlos had been in custody when the attacks took place and the mysterious Englishman was said to have run away with Carlos's daughter and had disappeared, and both their whereabouts were unknown.

Enquiries by the Spanish authorities failed to identify the Englishman from their records of students entering the country. Enquiries in the village brought conflicting results. Maria was recorded as a person of interest by the Guardia Civil and the trail went cold.

Chapter 4

قف علي, ناصية الحلم وقاتل,

Stand on the battlefront of your dream and fight for it.

Unbeknown to the students in London, the PLO leaders and Israeli diplomats had met once again, this time secretly. Their aim was to establish common ground for discussions on the situation in the Middle East, and to develop a formula to stop conflict in Israel and the Gaza Strip.

However, there had been much debate on the subject within Palestinian ranks, and details of the meeting had leaked out to the more militant factions within the movement. One of these groups decided that the time to talk had not yet come, but the opportunity to seize power within the organisation was presenting itself, if the talks collapsed. The standard way to achieve that, was by orchestrating an act of aggression, to induce a backlash from the Israelis. The suffering induced by the Israeli response, would lead to calls for a more robust approach, and thus play into the hands of the more militant factions.

The 'hawks' within the Palestinian movement were poised to take action. They would not of course get their hands dirty, and any 'military' action, would be carried out by the 'Fist of Islam.' The 'hawks,' would, of course, finance any action through funds diverted from collections and donations for the care of the 'orphans of Islam,' who would remain in rags, with dirty water in the refugee camps.

In a training camp in the Beqaa Valley, a group of militants was drawing up a plan. An armed group of 'martyrs' would take over the hotel, where the PLO leaders were to stay, and when the inevitable siege situation resulted, another 'martyr' would drive a car bomb as close to the hotel as he could get, and detonate it. The group would claim this bomb, was the work of the Israelis. The 'martyrs' in the hotel would then shoot the PLO 'doves,' and blow themselves up as Police, or the SAS, entered in a rescue mission. The claim would be made that the Israelis were trying to destroy all the future potential Palestinian leaders.

Inevitably there would be worldwide condemnation of the incident, as there would be British casualties. The Israelis would carry out reprisals, and the PLO, now run by militants, would say that Israel had no intention of bringing peace, without the destruction of Palestine.

The Training Officer of the 'Fist of Islam' looked at the room of young recruits, sitting in rows after prayers. He delivered a rousing speech calling on all the faithful to rise up in the name of Allah, to give themselves to the 'Holy War.' The room was whipped up into a frenzy of solidarity and fervour. He called on them to fulfil the ultimate sacrifice, to give themselves to Allah, so that successive generations could live in a world where love and peace would exist, under the banner of Islam.

In his mind the trainer had already chosen six young men, who he thought were ready mentally, to give themselves to be martyred, and in death, achieve the honour and respect of their families, though their mothers would weep for them.

A member from the group in London had arrived in the camp some days before, and reported on the group's resources there. He was instructed to set up more safe houses for the martyrs, and formulate plans for selected locations.

They had received details of the date of the meeting of the PLO leaders, well in advance of the staged conference. He said that a full out attack on the actual conference would be too risky, as the British and Israeli security would be too tight. The hotel was enormous, and he thought rooms could be booked in advance for the martyrs, possibly by British sympathisers claiming to be press. Once the rooms were booked, and the occupants were seen to be innocent, the martyrs could take their place at the last moment.

'We have been encouraging a group of English students, to be part of the Palestinian struggle, and they can be used, to create a diversion, and show the world, that our struggle has universal support. They'll set up a demonstration, and we have one of them ready and willing to place a series of devices. These people are expendable, they are not of the faith, and are only motivated by their own left-wing politics. They have a false notion of what the 'holy war' means, and as soon as it suits them, they would reject the cause. If they are arrested, it does not matter, in fact it would be good, as it would show the breadth of support for our cause. There is no risk, as they know nothing,' reported the group member.

The six chosen martyrs received a more detailed briefing, and were started on a more intensive programme of training and indoctrination built into prayer sessions.

The plan was for them to travel to North Africa, to Morocco, and then over to Spain, and up to a safe house in northern Spain run by people smugglers. They were taught how to make, and deploy, simple devices using component parts acquired for the group, and how to operate suicide belts, and rig up a suicide car bomb. They were instructed how to operate as a team in a foreign environment, with forged papers disguising their identity.

The group member who had just come from London, returned to London, and immediately contacted Roderick, instructing him to start constructing incendiary devices, and to contact Hilda and Pete, to arrange the student's demonstration.

He said 'tell them the PLO leaders, are trying to do a deal with the Israeli's, who are going to annex all the Palestinian homeland, and shift out the Arab inhabitants to refugee camps. The only ones, who will stay, will be those who renounce a free Palestine, in favour of a puppet state run by Israel. They are to stir up fellow students, and left-wing groups, to set up the demonstration. There are

Arab students too, who will support the demonstration, and go to any meetings where they are being arranged, monitor the situation, and report back. You will not attend in case there are traitors in our midst. Security prior to the action is essential. You are to keep a low profile at all times.'

The group member went on to explain to Roderick that the operation would be made up of a number of staged incidents, some of which Hilda and Pete's group were to be a part of. These incidents would be in support of a major operation run by a team, made up of soldiers of the 'Fist of Islam.' He was to brief Hilda and Pete at their flat, but after that, he was to keep contact with them down to the essential. He was not to mention to anyone, that the soldiers were coming to London.

In the days after he spoke to Roderick, the London based member of the group, set up a number of safe houses for the team, so they could split into pairs. Roderick was not told the location of these extra safe houses.

Roderick went round to meet Hilda and Pete, and duly briefed them along the lines outlined by the group member, leaving nothing out, hinting that any risky action would be taken by the groups 'Soldiers.' The conversation was picked up by the surveillance devices in the flat, and was heard by the Mossad agents in their van, and duly recorded. The conversation was analysed back at the embassy, and Michael's boss was visibly concerned.

He asked, 'who the hell is here now? Soldiers, smacks of them bringing in a team. I was sure they would not risk these clowns, doing anything spectacular, so I suppose it was only a matter of time, before a division one team moved in. But will they still use this flat for any support operation? We had better still monitor them. The students, with Roderick as the go between, are expendable, and they will just use them, so their real operatives, will not be seen by these students. We'll have to put a tail on Roderick, see where he goes, to whom he speaks. It's the only way at present, we have of identifying their team.'

'Sure boss, we don't know if they'll make up the improvised explosive mix in the flat, the chemicals are still there, so Roderick has to go there, to collect them. If this team has an explosives man with them, they will get him to make it up. Surely, they cannot risk the students trying to do it, they will blow themselves up, its terrible stuff,' said Michael.

'The timers are fixed, is that correct Michael?' asked his boss.

'Yes boss,' said Michael, 'and their instructions, from the group's main explosive man, is not to play with the devices, but if the team has an explosives man in the team, he could look at them. However, I think that is a small risk, they have a terrible history when it comes to electronics, their so-called experts are rubbish, so, we should still be ok. If anyone does work out there is a problem with the timers, they could send a soldier, to find out what is going on. We must watch the students, to see if they are threatened. We may have to take action to protect Habib, he would be the obvious target, for them to get answers. So, maybe, we should tell him to keep clear of the group.'

'It's essential we find their safe house, I am sure it will not be the same one Roderick is using. Michael, I agree, please brief our man Habib, tell him to be cautious, but don't let him know too much about the position, yet, just in case, they catch him out.'

'Ok, how do we play the British authorities, how much do we tell them?' asked Michael.

'My problem Michael, I will say we have intelligence that something is going down, but, that information is sketchy. If the students do any bombings, we will have to give them up.'

'And the demonstration?' continued Michael.

'They will know from activity at the campus, and when the students start to make up placards, that is a sure sign, a demonstration is imminent,' his boss said.

The Mossad were not the only ones who heard that another demonstration was planned, at the Mosque the Imam found out too. He overheard that an English couple, students at the North London College were whipping up support for a pro-Palestinian march, and a demonstration. He quickly established that the two students were Hilda and Pete, and they had involved a number of Arab students in their arrangements. So, he invited them to come to the mosque. They duly complied, and went to see him.

The Imam is a tall, slim man with greying beard and glasses, he has a gentle manner and invites Hilda and Pete, to sit, and take some tea with him.

'I am the Imam of this Mosque, and the spiritual father to all who attend here. I will come to the point directly, in the Koran there is no mention of Jihad. Allah is the supreme God, and can take care of his people without your help. I know you mean well, but you are putting yourselves at the risk of ruining your lives, for a struggle, that is not yours, please, do not get involved, stop what you are trying to do in the name of Islam, please, stop.'

'Well it's more in the name of free Palestine,' said Hilda.

'And you think you can affect, a struggle, that has been going on for hundreds of years?' said the Imam with a wry smile.

'We can support our brothers in Islam, as they take part in that struggle. We will stand in solidarity with the oppressed, of any society, isn't that a worthwhile thing?' said Hilda.

'Child, greater minds than yours are trying to work out the disputes between Arab and Jew,' the Imam added, with a little frustration. 'Force has not worked to date, to look at the problem peacefully, is the way forward. Talk and pray, and a solution will be found, in Allah's good grace?'

'But your enemies don't want peace, they just want to dominate, and seize the land of your fathers for their own,' said Pete.

'That is not true, Jew and Arab have lived together, for all time, the farmers in the field, don't want conflict, they have enough problems with the seasons. It is only the men who seek power, who look for strife, and adventurers, and romantics like you, who seek a thrill. I beg you walk away from any rash act. By all means support Islam, but in words, and not by the sword,'

'Thank you, we hear your words,' said Hilda.

'Well my son, my daughter, go in peace,' said the Imam.

They returned to the flat, where Roderick met them. They repeated the Imam's words to him.

'That is typical, there will be no change, unless there is action. He sees his cosy existence being disturbed if there is trouble, that's all,' said Roderick impatiently.

'I got the impression Roderick, that that old man knew more than he is letting on, is there something ,we should know?' asked Hilda.

'No, he is not in the loop,' snapped Roderick.

'But he found out about us soon enough,' said Pete.

'Not surprising, as you are trying to get students out on a demo, about Palestine,' said Roderick.

'Roderick I think we should be more careful. I don't like having all this stuff in the flat, what if we are raided by the Police?' said Pete.

'I am making up the mix now, and that is why I am here, it will be put into plastic boxes, and then removed to be wired up in the next day or so. So it will be out of here. Happy now?' said Roderick.

'It might be an idea to warn your contacts about what the Imam said, he will be repeating the message to people in the Mosque, and we have a number of Arab students helping us get support for the demo,' warned Pete.

'They may think about postponing their operation, let our demo do the work, without there being anything excessive done,' said Hilda. 'Do you know what they plan, and when?'

'No, when they are ready, and when another team is in place, I assume, they will act. It is all to do with another meeting between the PLO leaders and the Israelis, here in London. They have not given me any details,' said Roderick.

'Roderick this is getting really serious, and dangerous, and I am beginning to feel very uncomfortable, especially as we have no control over the end game,' said Hilda. 'For God's sake be careful, and let us know what they are planning to do.'

'Just relax, and do as they ask, they'll be taking the action, not us,' said Roderick.

With that Roderick left with a number of plastic boxes in carrier bags. As soon as he got to his flat, he phoned his handler in the group, and told him of the meeting between Hilda, Pete and the Imam and repeated Pete's observation, that the Imam could affect the Arab student's involvement in the planned demonstration. The handler's reply took Roderick a little by surprise.

'Silly old fool, why did he get involved, what did he say to them? He has to be told to keep his counsel, and not get involved. He could become a nuisance, so he'll have to be taught a lesson.'

That evening, as the Imam left the Mosque, he was set upon by a group of youths in balaclavas. He was badly beaten up, and a passer-by who tried to intervene, was also badly beaten, and left with the Imam, lying on the pavement. The two men were admitted to hospital, where it is found that the Imam had a fractured skull, and the 'Good Samaritan,' a local white English shopkeeper, had broken ribs. The youths had vanished before the Police arrived, and there were no witnesses to the incident. The 'Good Samaritan' had no idea what they looked like.

The press immediately jumped to the conclusion, that is was the work of the 'National Front,' and that was the story, carried in all the tabloids, despite a police statement, that they had no evidence that any political group was involved. The 'Fist of Islam' group made sure that the Arab community, were told that the British far right were responsible, and that they did the act in support of their Zionist allies.

Hilda and Pete accepted the media's version of events, and this re-kindled their resolve to have their demonstration, which they planned for Duckett's Common in Wood Green. They decided to bring the date forward, for more impact. However this did not fit in with group's timetable, and they could see events taking their own course and veering out of their control.

The Imam was unconscious for several days, but when he eventually gained consciousness and was interviewed, he said that he could not describe his assailants, other than to say they were young and strong. The local reporter tried to get him to say they were 'National Front,' or at least white, but he refused, saying he did not know.

'Allah is all seeing, and he will take care of any punishment that is needed, it is not for me to seek revenge, but to continue serving him.'

The newspaper did in fact print his words 'verbatim' and added his plea for calm. The attack was condemned by the British Government, in a broadcasted statement, while radical Islamic and 'Left Wing' group called for action.

Roderick completed the assembly of the devices, and delivered them in a box to a Lebanese restaurant in the West End. A young Middle Eastern looking couple, entered shortly after and ordered a meal. Two men sat outside the restaurant, in a car, watching the alley at the rear. An hour later a young Arab entered the restaurant via the front door, and a few minutes later emerged at the rear, and into an alleyway, he was now wheeling a motor bike, he had taken from the restaurants small loading area. Attached to the rear seat was strapped the box. He set off down the road, followed seconds later by the car. Another motorbike came in behind the car and followed the Arab's bike, while the car veered off down a side street.

The two motor bikes continued through the west end, towards Camden Town until the Arab stopped outside a butcher's shop, where he delivered the box. A small van, which had joined the small procession, sometime previous, stopped across the street. The following motorcycle continued on without stopping. One of the occupants of the van got out, and knocked on the door of a shop selling luggage, situated across the street from the butchers.

By a strange quirk of fate, the shop was run by a Jewish couple, the man had, in the past worked for the Israeli Embassy as security at Hebrew meetings. The man who knocked at his door convinced the shop owner to let him in, speaking quietly in Hebrew. Once inside he set up an observation point, in a bedroom, looking directly into the front of the butchers shop. This man was a Mossad agent.

The agent quietly cursed, as there was bound to be lots of comings and goings to the butchers shop with parcels being delivered and taken away. However no large containers were removed before the shop closed. The agent took over a dozen photographs of customers and employees, before the shutters came down. He then contacted the

Embassy for instructions.

'Our friend at the bag shop is ok with me being here, I have a good view of the front of this butcher's shop, but not of the rear, I think it goes into a mews, with one exit through an arch at the front, but I don't know if there is an exit to the street, at the rear, from the mews. Can you check?'

'Stay there, we are checking the map now. Ah, it is ok the mews has only one entrance at the front, presumably through the archway. We are finding out now, about the butcher, but surely it will not be long, before we should see someone we know. Checks are being made at the students flat, to see if the chemicals, at least, have gone. Stay where you are for the present, and we will get you a relief.'

When Hilda and Pete went to the demonstration, two Israeli gentlemen visited their flat, and found that the chemicals and other bomb making material, had in fact, been removed.

The demonstration in Wood Green was a lively affair, with plenty of chanting and placard waving. There was a moment of tension, when a few words were exchanged between the demonstrators and Arsenal supporters, on their way to the local 'Derby' match with Tottenham Hotspurs, fortunately the footballers were more interested in getting to the match, than with Palestinian politics. The cry as they vanished towards White Hart Lane rather incongruously was 'Yidd army, Yidd army, Yidd army,' which was met by a string of abuse about the Israeli's and their illegal occupation of Arab lands, which, fortunately was lost on the football supporters. There were no serious disturbances, as there was a large police presence.

Several arrests however were made as the demonstration was breaking up. A few locals, a little the worse for drink, left their pub to find students with placards, on what they considered to be their village green. The locals who included a couple of Jamaicans, mounted a counter demonstration. The theme of their anger appeared to be centred on continued immigration, especially Afghans, Iranians, and Iraqis and what they called 'left wing looneys' supporting the Kurds. Several placards got ripped from the student's hands and a small fight broke out, quickly stopped by the Police, who up to that point, had been bored stiff.

The press was in attendance and interviewed Hilda, giving her the opportunity to outline the Palestinian cause, and the suffering of their people at the hands of the Israeli army. When asked if she thought the Arsenal supporters were pro Jewish, she became rather truculent and told the reporters not to trivialise what was a serious issue.

At this point chanting was heard coming louder and louder and the reporters left to intercept the triumphant Arsenal supporters who had prevailed over their opponents. Hilda, and her close group of student supporters decided that they had seen enough confrontation for the day, and beat a hasty retreat down into the underground, leaving their placards littering the common.

The feedback from the 'Fist of Islam' by way of Roderick, was quite positive. They were pleased that the demonstration had made the TV news and the front pages of the tabloids, and had at least brought Middle Eastern politics back centre stage. The television clips were of the occupants of the pub fighting with the students. Fortunately, the drunk's voices were sufficiently slurred as to be almost inaudible. The reporter stated, above the din, that support for a free Palestine was growing. Hilda's interview was not broadcast in full, and she was left rather deflated.

'Well, I'm glad they are pleased, but, when will the press listen? If they can get it wrong, they will. I spelt it out for them quite clearly, and that was never broadcast. I give up!'

Roderick told them that the main event would be postponed, as there was a problem bringing in the 'Soldiers of Islam.' He added that when they arrived, and carried out their operation, the whole world would listen. He said there would be another meeting between the PLO leadership and the Israelis, later in the year, to finalise an agreement, this would give the group some time, to set things up properly. So for now they could relax. Roderick said he would not be coming back to the flat as Hilda would be identified, from the broadcast, as an activist.

His suspicions were well founded, as it was not long after he left them that another van joined the Mossad's van, this one was occupied by Special Branch surveillance officers. The local residents were now getting fed up with vans outside their front doors, as they had to go elsewhere to park their own vehicles.

Habib had watched the events from the relative safety of his uncle's house and inwardly breathed a sigh of relief, until he had a surprise visit from Roderick.

'I took one of the devices to the group, and they said it did not work. They got very annoyed. It must be their timer, all the other stuff is very simple, and I told them that. They said the timers, were standard units, that always worked. Can you fix it for me?' asked Roderick.

'From what I saw of the electronic technology, it is very basic, and the circuits are sealed in resin, which would make it virtually impossible, to do anything with. Look, Roderick, I just don't want to get involved,' said Habib.

'Well like it or not you are, it won't take the police long to connect you to the flat, and remember you were arrested following the shooting, they know you. Just do me a favour, and check out that timer.'

'Ok, but only bring the timer, I don't want any explosive stuff here,' said a reluctant sounding Habib.

Roderick went to a car and returned with a device, minus the charge.

Habib took a look, and shook his head.

'I will have to check this out at the University, I don't have the equipment here. You can see for yourself, it would be difficult, to get testing equipment probes onto the circuit, through that resin.'

'Ok, but please do your best, and let me know, as soon as you have.'

Roderick told the group that he is getting the timer checked out by an expert. His direct contact in the group got very annoyed until Roderick told him that the expert is an Arab, the man who was arrested after the shooting incident. He told him Habib's story, how his mother was killed when Israeli jets blew up an explosive store in the Lebanon, and that his sympathies did lie with their cause. The group discussed the development and told Roderick to keep in touch with the man, as he may become useful later.

At the university, Habib confided, once again, with Professor Randall and it was not long before Michael appeared. He asked to see the timer.

'Yes, it's a 'Jihad 1', they are normally quite reliable, but I think when you check it you will find the chip does not work, so the thing is useless. They are stuck, they can't repair it, because it's in resin,' said Michael.

'Why do they put the circuitry in resin?' asked Habib.

'It protects it, and stops their operatives fiddling about with it,' said Michael.

'Yes, ok, I can see that, but this one looks as though it has been deliberately blown, fried in fact. I have a horrible feeling, they are going to get me to check all of the timers, and, they will all be fired. What am I going to say to them?' asked Habib.

'We can play it two ways,' said Michael, 'let them think they work, when they don't, or, build up your credibility by saying they don't, and then you will tell them you will build some, that will work. You, and we, will then have control over making the new ones, and maybe, we can put some extra features on.'

'You knew they wouldn't work, didn't you?' said Habib looking into Michael's eyes.

'Habib, what I know about timers, could be written on a postage stamp,' was the reply.

'I bet you were in the Israeli Army, doing your national service?' said Habib.

'Yes, using properly made weapons, not this rubbish.'

'What do I tell Roderick?' asked Habib.

'Tell him the timers have been sabotaged, and he should get some new ones,' said Michael after a moment's thought.

'But he will ask me to make them,' said Habib.

'Yes, that is what we want, and it must be you who makes them. I know it is a dangerous game, but we will have to be able to track them,' said Michael.

'Ok, but I will need some help with this, and some insurance. I don't want to get arrested again,' said Habib.

'We can look after that aspect,' said Michael, 'have no fear on that account.'

Habib contacted Roderick and told him of his findings. Roderick immediately asked him to make new ones.

'I don't want to, but I know you will force me, or they will,' said Habib.

When Roderick came back to Habib, he told him that he does not have to make the timers.

'An engineer with the 'soldier group' that is coming here, will do that,' said Roderick.

He then shows Habib a shopping list of components and tools that the expert will require, and he asks Habib if he will help him acquire them. He also said he had to get a van for them, and arrange a safe house.

Michael was not concerned, but he wanted Habib to let him know as soon as Roderick had got a van, and where the safe house was going to be.

Habib duly helped Roderick purchase the electronic components and went with him to get the van. Roderick however did not confide in him where the safe house was. Habib reported back to Michael, who was immediately concerned.

'That is a nuisance, we are now playing that dangerous game I spoke of. The reward is, that we may be able to find out who the explosives expert is. Habib, do you know, where, Roderick took the electronic stuff, he bought. Some of the integrated circuits are for timers, as you well know. You say the sophisticated ones, you still have to purchase, is that right?'

'Yes, but I don't know, where the stuff he has bought went,' said Habib.

'Can you find out where these last components are going?' asked Michael.

'I will try, but he could get suspicious, if I ask too many questions.'

'Whatever you do, do not put yourself on offer. Look ,when you go to buy those components, let us know and we will do the rest,' said Michael.

'Ok, but those soldiers he keeps talking about, could they be the suicide bombers, we keep hearing about?' asked Habib.

'Who knows, they could be, which is why we are persevering with this option. By just letting them have dud timers will not help matters at this point, the suicide devices, do not need sophisticated electronic circuitry,' said Michael. 'The priority is finding out who the soldiers are, and who is making their devices. They will not use improvised chemical charges, that is for sure, they will bring in some form of military explosive, but what and how, those are the questions. I suspect the timers are for either a large vehicle bomb, or distraction devices?'

'But a large vehicle bomb, is going to cause death and

injury, to anyone that is in the area, surely?' said Habib.

'Yes, it's a dangerous game we play, as I have said before. So we have to be clever, when the timers are made, Habib, we have a few secrets up our sleeves, we can use, I assure you,' said Michael. 'I cannot say now what they are, you will have to trust us. We of course have to find those timers, before they are used, and, how shall I put it, modify them. Which is why it is a nuisance, they are getting their own man to make them.'

Michael arranged for a tracker to be put on the van that Roderick had bought, and a surveillance team followed Roderick and Habib, as they made their last few purchases.

As far as the 'Fist of Islam' were concerned, Roderick had got all the equipment they wanted, fixed the transport, and got a safe house that would remain empty till the 'soldiers' arrived. So, they waited for news from their contact in North Africa heralding the arrival of the 'Soldiers of Islam.'

Chapter 5

ما ندمت على سكوتي مره، لكنني ندمت على كلامي مرارا

I have never regretted my silence.
As for my speech, I have regretted it over and over again.

Rory and Maria arrived at the house of Uncle Luigi, situated in Santa Clara, a tiny village, of just a few houses and a bar, set deep in the Pyrenees and well off the tourist route. Uncle Luigi was a man in his late seventies who still found the energy to tend his small flock of some thirty sheep, however it was getting harder every year.

In addition to his small farmhouse he had a cabin, set in the woods well hidden from casual view. In this cabin he allowed all sorts of folk to stay, providing they paid in cash. It was sufficiently far away from his house that he never saw any of the people who stayed there, some of course were fugitives, and most had their stay arranged by a group loosely affiliated to ETA.

The cabin was showing some signs of wear and tear, because Luigi, in recent years, was not capable of carrying

111

the repairs as he would have wished. This was where he sent Rory and Maria. He said they could spend their time helping him with the sheep, and doing some work on the cabin to make it more comfortable. Because they were family, or at least Maria was, he would not charge them rent.

Rory slipped easily into the role of shepherd, and once he had got the trust of the old border collie sheepdog, a working relationship blossomed. In the first few weeks Rory and Maria cleaned up the interior of the cabin, and Rory mended a hole in the roof, replaced a window, repainted, and preserved the outer walls. Luigi was impressed with Rory and accepted him as a member of the family too. Maria had also softened towards Rory, and they had become a couple in the eyes of the locals, and in reality.

Maria asked if she could help in the little bar in the village, for a small wage, which gave them more independence. Luigi insisted on providing them with food and the odd bottle of wine. The weeks become a month and Rory finished all the renovations he could do, Luigi was really pleased and said they could stay as long as they liked, and he wanted Maria to inherit the cabin when he died.

The cabin had no electricity, and water was obtained from a mountain stream that ran a few yards from the door, cooking was done on a wood burner. Three small rooms formed one half of the cabin and the other half was open plan with the stove and a sink. Outside there was a crude shower, and a small hut for tools.

Deeper into the woods was a barn where straw and fodder was stored for the sheep. The trees were mainly conifer and provided a barrier from the outside world, and logs for the stove were stacked up against the rear wall. A small path through the woods lead to an open hillside overlooking the village, a kilometre away in the distance. The setting was a rural idyll, with the sheep on land owned by Luigi, just a few yards away. The peace and tranquillity did not last however, Luigi had some paying guests who needed the cabin urgently.

'There are six Arabs passing through, they want to stay for a few nights. I told them the cabin was occupied. The people who arrange these things, say they will stay in the barn, they will not mind. The men in charge are Basques I have known them a long time, they have never let me down, but as they say, there is always a first time.'

'These Arabs, they are on the run?' asks Maria.

'I don't know, I don't care, but I expect they are, they are friends of Fernando. He met them in the Lebanon. He says they are Palestinians, on their way to England,' said Luigi.

'They will be terrorists,' said Maria 'he will have met them at one of those training camps, in the Beqaa Valley. Pedro went there.'

'How long do they intend staying?' she asked.

'Two days, as I understand, before a lorry and a guide, will collect them, and take them to the coast. I assume they will then go on a trawler over to England, that is the normal way,' said Luigi.

'Whose trawler' asked Maria?

'It's the Santa Anna,' he replied.

'Oh no, it's repaired then?' she asked.

'Yes, has been for a little while now,' he said.

'Who is using it now?' Maria asked, with a worried expression.

'Pedro Fernandez,' sighed Luigi.

'I thought it might be, he is one of Rodriguez's men,' said Maria. 'Get rid of them, as quick as possible, if news that we are here gets to that man, we are in trouble. It was them, who set up Carlos, they planted the drugs in Carlos's boat.'

'I never knew, I heard that Carlos was in trouble, but no details. The Arabs will be here in a couple of hours, I can't stop them, now,' said Luigi.

'Will any of Rodriguez's men be with them?' she asked.

'Only the guide, and of course, Pedro Fernandez, who will take them down to the boat, but that will be at night, I think tomorrow night,' said a worried Luigi.

'How do you know this,' demanded Maria.

'Pedro came here to set it up. He told me. I said they must stay at the barn, as I had a shepherd in the forest house. He did not want you involved, as you may talk. He is going to try, to keep the Arabs inside the barn, as he does not want them wandering around, and annoying the locals.'

'Does Pedro know Rory and I are here?' she asked.

'Not that it is you, no,' said Luigi. 'I don't think they have made the connection between you and me, but I think it is best, if you take Rory up into the high pasture, and Maria you had better not go to the bar, either stay out with Rory, or in the house here with me.'

'I will go and spend a night with Rory under the stars, and we will not go back into the cabin, until they have gone, there is a shelter up on the high pasture I know, we will be ok,' she said, as much to allay her own fears as Luigi's.

The Arabs arrived three hours later in a large lorry, which had great difficulty getting along the narrow road to the village. They were all young men, and they had travelled for hours in the back of the vehicle, after spending two hours in a false compartment under the lorry, while they passed through border controls. When they were told they had to spend the night in a barn, they were not happy.

The guide told Luigi 'they are complaining about having to go in a barn, as they have been cramped all day. They say they have paid Rodriguez good money already, and don't feel they should be treated this way.'

'It's best they stay in the barn, it is dangerous to wander about as the Guardia Civil have patrols in the hills, and the villagers are a suspicious lot. I will make it comfortable for them,' said Luigi. 'When will I get paid, for the food and the risks I am taking for these people?'

'When Pedro comes to take them away,' said the guide.

Luigi took the group up to the barn, he collected blankets stored in the cabin, on the way and set up a crude table, on which he set out food. The Arabs relaxed and smiled at Luigi. The guide did not speak Arabic, but one of the Arabs spoke a little Spanish, and thanked Luigi.

Maria kept hidden away till Luigi returned to his house. He said that the guide had gone, and the Arabs were settled in the barn. Luigi had told the guide, he was not happy with the arrangement, and he wanted his money.

'The truth is Maria, I just want them gone, I am not

bothered about the money, but, I am worried now, as that Rodriguez is a sneaky, evil man and I would not rule out, the possibility he would tell the Guardia, and get a reward, they are not Spanish, so who would care if they were arrested,' said a clearly worried Luigi. 'You can bet that the Arabs will not have seen him, the only one taking any risks will be Pedro, and he will not identify Rodriguez. The Arabs are calling Pedro 'Pepe,' so he is taking precautions as well. I think it is best you go up in the high pasture, to the shelter, and keep away from the cabin for a while.'

'I will sneak into the cabin now and get our papers and passports, and keep them with us, just in case it all goes wrong,' said Maria.

'I think you are wise, it's best to be prepared, and I have some money here, take it,' said Luigi, handing over a roll of notes. 'If you have to run, I will have some of your things ready, if you have a chance to come back here. I will go and get them from the cabin now.'

Maria kissed Uncle Luigi before she left moving quickly and silently up into the hills, after a quick visit to the cabin. She listened for the Arabs, but could hear no sound, and she presumed they were asleep after their arduous journey. She found the flock and Rory in the high pasture and updated him on the position. He agreed it was prudent to have taken precautions.

They sat with the dog while the sun set over the mountains, turning them through a range of blues, greens, yellows and finally a deep red before the sun vanished, and was replaced by a stream of stars arcing across the firmament. The moon was a thin crescent, preserving the blanket of sparkling darkness. They chatted for quite some time about the meaning of life, before huddling down in the shelter, while the dog lay outside as a guard, not only of the sheep, but of his human companions.

The next morning the sun rose through a yellow haze, and slowly revealed a peaceful mountain scene, with green slopes flowing away from a line of fir trees, through which poked rocky outcrops against the background of a cloudless pale blue sky. The sheep munched contentedly or lay quietly staring at nothing. This scene of rural tranquillity was watched over by a shepherd, his girl, and their dog, until it was shattered by four horsemen suddenly appearing, two along the valley below where the couple sat, one from the trees, and one up the slope from the village.

The horsemen were in green uniforms with black tricorn hats. One swung his horse sharply into the section of trees, that hid the barn from view, as if he had seen someone lurking there. He had just gone out of view behind the screen of trees, when there was a sharp crack, that echoed down the valley. The horse appeared riderless and, as if in two minds, stopped. The other horsemen urged their steeds up the slope and into the trees where their colleague had gone. One took out a rifle from its long cover and dismounted, moving cautiously through the trees, he was quickly joined by the other two, one on foot the other still mounted.

The shepherd and his girl moved to behind a large rocky outcrop, and crouched down looking towards the trees. The sheep had looked up briefly before continuing to munch at the grass. The dog crouched with the couple, silently waiting for instruction.

A series of sharp cracks echoed around the trees, before three horses bolted out into the open and joined the fourth, before hurtling all together down the slope. On one of the horses a Guardia Civil officer hung precariously from the saddle. A man followed on foot and fired at the retreating horse. He saw the couple and came directly over to them.

He pointed his gun at Rory and in broken Spanish said, 'You speak English?'

'Yes,' replied Rory.

'We go now, you drive the lorry' and he pointed the rifle at Maria.

Rory replied 'the police will be here soon, you will never drive that thing fast enough on these roads to outrun the police. You will never get away in that lorry.'

'No, you go!'

'The police knew you were here, they were obviously tipped off. We cannot afford to have them find us here now, they will arrest us too. The man who organised this will make trouble for us,' said Maria.

'What should we do?' said the man in a frightened voice.

'You will be better off, sending the lorry down the slope, so it crashes and burns up, so they think you have crashed, they will spend a lot of time getting to it, and with this time, you can escape over the hills,' suggested Rory.

'I don't know the way,' said the man.

'We do and can guide you,' said Maria.

'Why you do this for me?' he asked.

'You have been duped by men, who are our enemies too,

they have got your money, and set you up, come on there is little time, we have to move' said Maria 'and now!'

They reversed the lorry round onto the track, and along to a sharp bend in the roadway, where there was a steep drop down to a rocky slope, leading to a valley and the river. They set the vehicle across the road, started the engine, engaged a gear, and pushed the accelerator causing it to lurch over the edge and through the air till it hit the rocks. In a series of thunderous crashes the vehicle bounced down the slope, till it burst into flames, and exploded.

'Now we must move, through the trees fast, keep in cover. We will hide till nightfall, and then decide what to do,' said Maria.

They had not been far, before they heard the unmistakable sound of a helicopter flying low down the valley. It came to the site of the burning vehicle and circled as close as it could. The vehicle appeared to be caught on a ledge just over halfway down the rocky slope. Black smoke now replaced the flames, curling upward to meet the down draught of the rotor blades causing it to swirl, spiral and then dissipate in the mountain air.

'We go now, as far as we can, away, follow the line of the gully, it's hidden by trees. We are heading for a little hermit's cave I knew as a child, we can stay there till night, quick, move,' said Maria.

They followed Maria without comment as she led them along the gully, a rocky stream ran gently downward, the sides of the slopes leading away were steep and covered with thick vegetation. They could not move fast but they were almost invisible from the air. The helicopter was concentrating on the burning wreck, before it started a search of the open slopes, so they need not have worried about being spotted. The gully was joined by another stream, running into it, and they started to climb again reaching a rocky ledge which led to the cave.

The cave was only a few kilometres from the village but hidden from view. They waited there till night fall, and then returned to the junctions of the streams, and followed down a sharp incline. An overgrown path dotted with rocks took them further down, progress was slow in the darkness, Rory and the Arab lad stumbled many times, before they arrived at pastureland, which led directly to Luigi's door.

They stumbled into Luigi's kitchen where he was sitting in the dark.

'I heard the explosions, the Police have been trying to climb the rock face to the wreckage, I have been praying all day you were not in the vehicle. I heard the gunfight up at the barn, but I don't think they have been there yet.'

'Uncle we are not hurt, we were not involved, but we have an Arab with us, Mohammed. He said four police-men came to the barn, they came quietly and one of the Arabs, who was standing outside on guard opened fire on them. He shot dead two before they could do anything, then one of the others fired back. His other friends came out of the barn and they were all shot. He stayed inside and shot one of the other policemen when he tried to enter the barn. The fourth was still on his horse and he shot him too, when he could not get the rifle from the case, but he thinks he was just wounded. The horse galloped away, with that man still hanging in the stirrups.'

'I have not been anywhere near the barn, were any of his friends wounded?' asked Luigi.

'No, he looked, all the Arabs are dead, and the three policemen too, he alone is alive. The horses moved away together, along the slope, we think away from the village and the barn, but we are not sure. The Guardia was still hanging from the horse, so we do not know if he is alive or dead. I think he must be badly injured and most likely he will not have been able to tell them much about what happened, yet,' said Maria.

'It looks like they were tipped off to go to the barn, they would not have expected the Arabs to be armed, or there would have been more of them. It will have been that shit Rodriguez, or one of his men who told them. The Guardia must know where their men were headed, surely. I think they'll wait till morning light, before they continue their search, they will fear an ambush. They will not know if any of the Arabs are still there. I have been sitting here quiet, listening, and have heard nothing, they have not been here to me yet. But tomorrow, they'll come here in numbers,' said Luigi.

'We can't know what Rodriguez has told them, he may have told them I was there too, with Rory. Oh, damn, we will have to go!' said Maria.

'I think the best chance for us to go will be now, I can drive you down the old path. It will be dangerous, we cannot use lights. We'll join the old mountain road, well away from here. Few know the way, we should be safe,' said Luigi.

'Won't they set up roadblocks?' asked Rory.

'Not that far away, it's unlikely. It's a gamble, but one we can reasonably take,' said Maria.

'If they have seen the bodies at the barn, and seen the car crash, they will think most of the Arabs are dead or wounded, and not in a fit state to try an escape. Now, we cannot wait, we must move now. Does your new friend speak any Spanish?' asked Luigi.

'A little and some English too, he will have to follow what we plan,' said Maria.

'I go with you, I have no other way to get safe' said Mohammed. 'You, will take me?'

'Yes, come it is going to be a rocky ride. Once we are on the mountain road, we can get to the motorway, and I'll take you to Bilbao, you can hide better in the city. I'll have to be back here before sunrise, as it will not be long, before they are knocking on my door. I can put them off your scent, have no fear. But where will you go from Bilbao, you will not be able to stay there for long?' asked Luigi.

'You get me to a ship for North Africa, and I take you to my group, they can arrange for you to change identity, and move somewhere safe. I promise I will help you, if you help me,' said Mohammed.

They all piled into Luigi's car and he sped off across the fields to the track, and started following it slowly. There was only the thin crescent moon, so visibility was not good, and the journey was very uncomfortable. The old mountain road was a little better, and had a few good stretches, but there were, still, many potholes. Luigi confessed he was driving with his heart in his mouth.

It took just over two hours till they hit the motorway, and they were soon in the outskirts of Bilbao, where they said their farewells. Uncle Luigi in tears hugged Maria, and told Rory to look after her. Mohammed thanked him profusely and promised to say a prayer to Allah, for his safety, on the return journey.

'Oh I am taking the main roads, they won't be looking for anyone coming in the opposite direction,' he laughed before he sped away, just before the sun rose.

The sad trio clutching their bags, went and sat in a nearby park till the sun rose. They found a café and had some rolls and coffee with builders from a nearby building site. Mohammed said he had papers and a passport and could not see a problem getting into Algeria. He was glad to hear that Rory and Maria had papers too. He said the group would show their gratitude for helping him, he had plenty of money as he had grabbed his group's funds, before he fled the barn. Money for ferry fairs would not be a problem, and they would be able to stay in hotels.

Mohammed suggested the best way, would be to go with the tourists on the ferry from Algeciras to Ceuta and then into Algeria and along the coast to Algiers. They all duly took a bus to the railway station. and caught a train for Madrid. On arrival they booked into a hotel and Mohammed made several attempts to contact his friends without success. So they stayed for another day in Madrid, and Rory and Maria visited the Prada and the Reina Sofia. Eventually Mohammed was successful, and they were able to finalise their plans to get to Algiers.

After breakfast they purchased more clothes, and some

conventional luggage and generally accumulated the paraphernalia of tourists. It was indeed fortunate, that Mohammed appeared to have unlimited funds. They caught the train to Algeciras and were in time to take a ferry to Ceuta, and entered Morocco without any problem, as hordes of migrants were going the other way.

Once inside the country, Mohammed hired a car and they drove along the coast to the city of al Saidia and from there to the port of Bin Mahdi, near Ghazawat in Algeria. Mohammed contacted his group, and they arranged for a guide to meet him.

Relations between Morocco and Algeria have been strained for years, and there were difficulties that had to be overcome, in order to cross the land border, the negotiations were definitely clandestine, and Rory and Maria sat as passive onlookers, while the guide and Mohammed conversed quietly with the border guard, and after an envelope was passed to him, which he swiftly tucked in his pocket, they continued on. Once safely in Algeria, the guide left them.

They followed the line of the Tell Atlas Mountains parallel to the Mediterranean till they arrived in Algiers. Mohammed quickly made contact with his group and they were directed to a house in the district of Bab El Oued. They were to find out later it is famous for its square with 'the three clocks' and for its 'market.' It is predominantly an area of workshops and small manufacturing plants, with many narrow winding streets. It was in one of these streets they stopped at a terraced house.

The couple inside greeted them and hastily made a meal

for them consisting of couscous with chicken, carrots and chickpeas which was quite spicy. They had just finished the meal when three men joined them. They were part of Mohammed's group. It was clear they wanted an in depth briefing on what had happened in Spain. Mohammed got quite animated when he told them about Rodriguez, and the way that he had double crossed them. He told them that once he had their money, he set them up to be arrested, and this led to the gun battle.

They then turned their attention to Rory and Maria, and it was clear they were not happy that they were there. Mohammed told them how they had helped him escape, and that they were good people, who could be trusted. They too, were engaged in a struggle for the sovereignty of their country. He added that it was an odd quirk of fate, that he had met Rory, who was a qualified electronics engineer. He could help them produce some reliable devices, now that their engineer had been killed in the gun battle.

'He also has knowledge of improvised explosive devices, his uncle is a member of the Irish Republican Army and they have had people at the camps in the Beqaa Valley,' said Mohammed.

'We know, we have seen them there, but why would he help us?' one of the men demanded.

'They want to get back to London, with false identities, so they can start their life again,' said Mohammed.

'It is true, something has gone wrong with the timers in London, they have always been so reliable. We do not understand it. So for money and fresh papers, he will help us?' the man asked.

'Yes,' said Mohammed.

'Why should we trust them, look what happened with that Rodriguez man,' another one of the group asked.

'Without their help I could not have got this far, we have been through a great deal together, I trust them. They are not motivated by greed, they, with Allah's help, want to make a peaceful life. They had one in Spain, he was a shepherd, till that man ruined it for them, and they have become fugitives with me,' said Mohammed.

'What do they know about us?' asked the man, clearly the leader of the group.

'They know we are fighting for a free Palestinian state, that we are all members of the 'Fist of Islam,' that we are freedom fighters for Allah, that we serve him and him alone?' said Mohammed.

'And they understand that?' he demanded.

'Yes' said Mohammed.

'Right we will get this man to show us what he can do, then we will provide the papers for him to get to London, but not till he has proved his worth, you make that clear to him now,' the leader said firmly.

Mohammed relayed the conversation to Rory.

'How will I do this?' asked Rory.

'I will take you to shops selling electrical stuff, and you will be able to buy what you want' said Mohammed.

'I will need tools, and you must tell them, that what I make will be crude, but it will work,' said Rory.

'They know that,' said Mohammed 'it is just a test, in London they have all the up-to-date components, and tools there, so we won't need to carry any incriminating items with us, when we journey to London. They have a house for us there, so you will be safe.'

'Can you tell them, that we do not wish to get caught up, in what you are doing? We do not wish to place any bombs for you, is what I mean,' said Maria.

'No, they realise that, they are happy that you don't get that involved. Just make their devices work that is all. It is our struggle and we can fight the war successfully, with Allah's help,' said Mohammed.

They spent two uneventful weeks in Algiers. The family they stayed with were kind and hospitable and they had comfortable beds and were fed well. Maria was accepted as Rory's wife. A member of the group went with them when they purchased the items, that Rory needed, to make the simple timing devices. He made both long and short delays, and tested them so they could see they worked. He showed the man who shadowed him, how he could make them himself, and they were suitably impressed with his skill.

In another part of the city the group prepared Spanish passports for both Rory and Maria, and new papers for Mohammed. There was the odd visit from other members of the group, who now accepted them as allies. The couple who hosted them continued to look after them well.

The bond between Rory and Maria became even stronger and had moved to one of genuine love. It was a totally different experience for Rory living within an Arab community, the street scenes with the narrow dusty streets, the smells of spices pervading the air, the general noisy hustle and bustle, but he soon relaxed and embraced it. To Maria it was far more familiar, they helped around the house, but always went with one of their hosts, when they had to leave the immediate neighbourhood. The near neighbours soon got to know the couple, and would smile and exchange greetings, Rory learnt a few stock phrases in Arabic, and greeted them in the classic Arab fashion, which always met with approval.

Mohammed was an enigma to Rory, he was quiet and shy, and consumed with religious fervour. He did not expect Rory and Maria to follow the Islamic codes, but explained that prayer, 'Salah,' was one of the five pillars of Islam that he, Mohammed, had to follow. Before prayer he said he must perform 'wudu' to ensure he was ritually pure, which meant his body, clothes and that the place he knelt to pray on was cleansed, and always he must turn to face towards the 'Holy Ka'bah' the holy mosque in Mecca. He truly believed that communication with Allah through the Qur'an would bring him courage to face the world, and ensure that he conducted his life in the service of Allah, to glorify his name.

'Before we pray, Rory, we must have in our heart a purity, so we can enter into communication with Allah, which is the greatest blessing we could have,' explained Mohammed.

Rory remembered his words as they were to serve as an explanation for the tragic events, yet to come. He had a deep respect for Mohammed and his conviction, and saw that he was always respectful towards Maria. In his own way he was pleasant company, and had a good sense of humour. However, there seemed to be an underlying sense of tragic events in the past that he only hinted at. He was violently anti-Israeli, and said that he would give his life to ensure a free Palestinian State, run in the name of Allah, and not to the dictates of politicians, who had agendas of their own. He was well educated and spoke passable Spanish, and was fluent in English and French.

When the time came to leave, they decided they would go by ferry to Marseilles, and then take the train to Paris where they stayed overnight and the following day. They acted as tourists and Rory and Maria went to the Louvre and visited the west bank of the Seine. The following day they caught the train to Calais, where they took the ferry on to Dover.

At Dover they entered separately and it was Rory and Maria who were questioned about their reasons for coming to England. Their visits to the art galleries in Madrid and Paris proved to be a good investment, as they convinced the immigration staff they were there to study art in particular they wished to visit an exhibition of Monet's work in the National Gallery, which Rory had seen advertised on a poster displayed in the ferry. They opened their bag with books on Picasso and Miro which was enough to allay the immigration man's suspicions. Mohammed just said he was there to visit relatives in North London and went straight through.

Once past immigration and customs they continued to London by train and on arrival they went directly to their rendezvous point with the group at a Costa Coffee shop close to Victoria Station. They sat at a table on the pavement area and engaged in some silent people watching until they were approached by their contact from the 'Fist of Islam.'

'Mohammed is that really you, it's Abdullah, so good to see you, and you are Mohammed's friends, we have heard a lot about you. Come on Mohammed introduce me.'

'Rory and Maria, without them I would not be here today,' said Mohammed.

Abdullah smiled, but cut him short.

'You must be worn out, let's go, we must get you to your flat. We have to take the underground, and then we will pick up your car, is that ok.'

'Yes perfectly, so good of you to meet us,' said Rory.

'You will be comfortable there, the flat is just out of town, in fact you could almost say it's countryside,' chuckled Abdullah.

In the train he asked Rory about his qualifications in the field of electronic engineering and said he would set him up in a job, and winked. They took the Piccadilly line to Southgate, where they went to another café.

'We will meet again soon I hope. Now, a man called Roderick will join you, he has the keys for the flat and the car. The car is ours, and the flat is all paid up, so no need to worry.' Abdullah blew a kiss to Maria and was gone.

They waited for about half an hour, before they were joined by Roderick. He duly introduced himself, supplied them with the keys, and told them where their car had been left, and the index number, and gave them directions to the flat. He told them that he was deeply involved with the group, who relied on him to arrange so many things, and that it was not a good thing that he stayed in their presence for any longer than was necessary. Rory and Maria exchanged glances and Mohammed sensing their concern, said it was a wise precaution.

'There's a computer in the flat, and the next contact, from either me or the group, will be by e-mail. Now, there is a false back to a cupboard, which I constructed, and here is a note, of how to get into the space behind, destroy the note, when you have worked it out, ok,' said Roderick, as he spoke he looked around dramatically, as if looking for an enemy.

'Yes we will,' said Rory, with another look at Maria.

'Please enjoy your stay,' said Roderick, before looking up and down the street once more and then, going to his car.

'Mohammed, I wonder where they got him from?' said Rory.

Mohammed laughed, 'My friends said not to trust him, he has only been told, what he needs to know to do his allotted jobs, he is what you call a gofer, I think.'

'As always you are so polite, but I get the hint,' said Rory.

In spite of their reservations, all was as Roderick had said. They followed the directions, to what transpired to be a small semi-detached house in Potters Bar. Intrigued by the false back to the cupboard, they opened it to find a good-sized void in which there was a range of electronic tools and components. Maria went out and stocked the food cupboard and refrigerator, and they settled to a meal, and to contemplate what the future held for them. Mohammed said he would be leaving them to live else-where, as he had a specific role to play, and did not wish to put them in any unnecessary danger.

Maria had been worried about what might have happened to Uncle Luigi, but he was a wily old fox and he had age on his side. The Guardia clearly thought his years and infirmity ruled him out of any participation in the gun battle at the barn. He told them that because of his arthritis, he could not get up to the building these days, as often as he wanted, and had no idea who had used it. He said that Rodriguez would take advantage of his nature to use the building for his purposes, and probably the best thing for them, was to ask him who the people were. He said it was a great shame, but his shepherd was a really good lad, and a hard worker, and he was really upset he had left. The police asked what had happened to his niece, and he told them she had been so alarmed at what happened, she did not wish to stay in the area any longer, and had left with the lad, who was her boyfriend. He had no idea where they had gone.

The Guardia said that Rodriguez had told them that he was responsible for bringing the Arabs there, but had no idea what they wished to do. When he became suspicious that they were up to no good, he notified the Guardia. Luigi told them that Rodriquez was an evil criminal who would sell his grandmother for a profit if he could. He said he had told him to keep away from him, his house, and the barn, but he never listens and does not care, when it suits him he will use anyone, even you, the Guardia Civil.

One of the old Guardia knew Luigi, and he called him an old rogue, but at heart he knew him to be a good man, and he said there and then, that Luigi was probably right, but they could prove nothing, as Rodriguez knew too many people who would protect him.

Carlos appealed against his conviction for drug running, and a number of witnesses came forward to say that he had never been involved with drugs and was actively against their use. A local Guardia had spoken up for him too, and he was duly released and returned to the restaurant.

One lunchtime an Arab, after he had had some tapas, asked to speak to Carlos in private. They both went into the kitchen, where the man told Carlos that Maria and Rory were safe, and well, and with friends. He went on to say that he had a debt to settle with a man called Rodriguez, could he identify him. Carlos said he would rather have nothing to do with the man, who was evil through and through. The man said he was aware of that. Carlos suspecting that this man was no friend of Rodriguez, and told him to come to the restaurant the following evening, and he would point him out.

Carlos got a friend to tell one of Rodriguez's men that Miguel Sanchez, a known 'fence,' was asking for Rodriguez as he had something that would interest him, and he knew he could do him a favour for a small price. Rodriguez took the bait and came to the restaurant. Carlos was actively hostile towards him, and asked him not to stay. This request was ignored by Rodriguez, but not by the Arab who sat in another alcove. He nodded to Carlos indicating he had seen his quarry. Rodriguez stayed for an hour in what was a hostile environment, as other customers made it clear they did not appreciate his presence. Eventually he got fed up and cursing Carlos, he left, followed by the Arab.

As Rodriguez walked to where his car was parked, he felt something in his back and then heard a soft voice tell him, that he would shoot him there and then if he tried anything. The man told him they were going to a red car down the street, and then they would go for a little ride, as he had somethings to discuss with him. Rodriguez said he had better not try anything stupid, as he had influence, and would cause him a great deal of trouble. The Arab jabbed the gun hard into his back and told him to move. The two got into the car where another Arab sat in the driver's seat.

The car was driven out of the town and up to a spot overlooking the sea, where there was a small shrine to the 'Madonna and Child.' The Arab told him to get out and kneel before his God, and ask for forgiveness of his sins. Rodriguez realising the seriousness of the situation, started to offer money, and pleaded for his life. The Arab calmly shot him through the top of his head and stuck a sticker on what was left of his forehead. The sticker bore the logo of the 'Fist of Islam.'

Chapter 6

إيمانك يجب أن يكون أكبر من خوفك

Your faith has to be greater than your fear.

A second formal meeting between the PLO leaders and the Israeli Foreign Ministry was scheduled for London. Extracts of a leaked document were published in a couple of tabloids, declaring that there would be an amnesty for the PLO, and outlining what in effect was the creation of a puppet state. There would have to be a loss of Arab held land, where there was a dispute with Israelis. This was met with opposition from most other Palestinian groups, and there was no formal agreement announced by the PLO.

The 'Fist of Islam' in a broadcast statement, declared that it was a sell-out, that there must be a free Palestinian State, with no loss of land, and no strings attached. They also demanded an amnesty for all Palestinian activists.

Abu Salem, the leader of the 'Fist of Islam' group convened a meeting of his close followers. He declared it was essential that the true believers reinforced his message, and that his message must be heard all over the world.

In a separate meeting later, attended by his inner circle, he said their plans would have to be advanced, and modified to fit the change in circumstances.

Abu Salem said, 'the students are to arrange another demonstration for a set time and date. This time will coincide with the activation of pre-set devices, working on long delay pre-programmed timers. There would be multiple injuries to the demonstrators calling for a free Palestine, and the blame will fall on Israel. We will denounce Israel and call for immediate action to establish an Islamic free Palestine run by us.'

'There will bound to be a denial from Israel, and a backlash in Palestine. What will the British think if their citizens are injured or killed, we will have to make sure that our own security is tight? Those students are in no way reliable, they are unbelievers, they are just adventurers who would turn on us. How reliable is this foreign engineer making the devices?' asked a member.

'The new engineer is making the devices that is all. Once he has fulfilled his purpose he can be disposed of, if he causes trouble. We know he just wants to set up a new life, and does not wish to get involved, so he will not ask too many questions,' said Abu Salem.

'There is a second string to our bow. Now, as you know a supporter of ours, Abdullah Ibrahim is playing a double role, he is considered a moderate, he is a wealthy man who has the confidence of the PLO leadership, and is respected here in British diplomatic circles. He will invite one of the

PLO leaders to a meeting with him. At that meeting we will present him with our demands, which will include the release of our members held in custody. The PLO man will be forced to make a video denouncing the meeting with Israel. If he refuses, he will be put up for ransom. If there is an attempt to rescue him, a volunteer Mohammed, who will be with him all the time, will activate a suicide vest.'

'Will Ibrahim play along with this?' asked another member.

'He will be kept on side, if need be we will take his daughter as hostage for insurance. If all goes well she can be released. He can then say he was under pressure to accede to our demands, and he will be reinstated back into his original place,' said Abu Salem with a smile.

'I am still unhappy about the students, how close are they to us?' asked the same member.

'They know nothing of our real plans, they think they want to help Palestine, let them have their dreams and delusions,' said Abu Salem. 'But, you must realise, they have done much to publicise our cause already. However, we have a cut off, called Roderick, he can be disposed of if there is trouble, and he will be blamed as the left-wing radical he is. This new engineer we have, is called Rory, he is an IRA terrorist, who will work with Habib, another engineer who is less skilful with devices, however Habib is an Arab and will keep an eye on Rory.'

'What do we have to do now?' asked the member.

'There will be high grade explosives for the distraction devices and the suicide vests, and any other device, we want to place, either at the meeting, or at the PLO's hotel.

These will have to be prepared. Roderick will know nothing of this, or certainly, at this stage. This will mean the devices we use, can be more compact, and this will give us greater flexibility,' said Abu Salem.

'We have to be sure of our security, the British Police, Special Branch, will be sure to watch the students, especially since they are on their radar already. Do the Israelis have anyone here?' asked another member.

'Not that I am aware of, there is no love lost between London and Jerusalem at the moment, the British have a deep-seated mistrust of the Israeli authorities, which goes back to the Palestinian Mandate,' was Abu Salem's reply.

'I know but a lot has happened since then. Israel is backed by America and the British will go along with what they say. We will still have to be wary of the Special Branch, we know they have informants,' said the member.

'We do have that covered,' said Abu Salem, with a smile. 'Abdullah has a friend, who is a Special Branch superintendent, and, he works on the Middle East desk. This man thinks Abdullah is an informant, and he has been fed information and disinformation from us. This man talks a lot to Abdullah, so we hear a great deal from him. We know that he is attracted to Abdullah's wife Fatima, she is a beautiful woman and a slut. She is also attracted to me, and will do anything I ask her. She is inviting the superintendent to see her, while her husband is away, she'll drug him, seduce him, and take photos. We will, then, have him in our pocket, and can get any early warning of any major action, or any move by the students and possible interference from Israel.'

'Well I guess there is little more we can ask, we will have to pray to Allah that all goes well,' said the member, matching the smile of Abu Salem.

'Always' said Abu Salem and closed the meeting.

Roderick duly called on Rory, and said his contact wanted a number of timers with delays of several days so they could be activated at a specific time and date. Rory told him he would need different components, so Roderick went back to the group with a list that Rory had supplied him. They said they would get them by mail order, using an Arab, who ran a 'computer game' firm. By doing it this way, they would not attract any undue attention. The last thing they would want, was Roderick or Rory hunting around electronic shops.

Roderick was then tasked with finding a 'lock up' facility, he was instructed to pay cash and use a false name, and obtain a cage within the facility. He was to supply the group with duplicate keys for the locks. He quickly got the storage cage and with it the duplicate keys and passed them on to his contact giving him details of the name used, so he could have access too, at a moment's notice if need be.

Roderick pointed out that he was taking all the risks and wanted to be compensated. After a short meeting, the group decided to pay him extra. They said they wanted him to make sure Rory did his job properly. Roderick expressed his gratitude, and reaffirmed he would not let them down.

A week later a consignment of colourful ceramic plates and another of abstract metal sculptures arrived at the lock up, and were placed inside by Roderick's contact, who said he was an employee of the man who hired the lock up. He had the right key, so watched by the caretaker, the crates were moved inside.

The ceramic plates were made of high explosive, moulded into shape, and then covered with a coat of white paint, which was decorated with a colourful, Arabic design. The metal sculptures took the form of numerous abstract designs, and included in their makeup thin tubes which held commercial detonators.

Mohammed was still in the house with Rory and Maria, and remained his quiet reserved self. Maria became more and more curious as to what his intended role was, when asked his reply at first puzzled her.

'It's Allah's wish that I give myself to him as the ultimate sacrifice.' She discussed the reply with Rory who said.

'It's obvious to me Maria, that he is a suicide bomber, you hear about those people all the time in the Middle East now.'

'Surely he must realise he is being used?' said Maria.

'You can see how religious he is, and that is clouding his judgment. I doubt if he sees it that way,' said Rory, shaking his head.

'Rory he is such an innocent, we should talk to him,' said Maria.

'Maria in a lot of respects this situation applies to us too, we too are being used,' said Rory.

'Yes but we are not going to commit suicide. He is,' said Maria.

The opportunity for a quiet chat arose, one evening, and they asked him to consider who benefits from his sacrifice, without saying directly they knew he was likely to be on a suicide mission.

'Mohammed, the men who are urging you on, are the ones who benefit, and what they want is political power, and standing, within their community, it's not for the sake of religion. They will never put themselves in the way of any harm, because they have got you, to do it for them,' said Maria quietly to him.

'They are giving me the opportunity, to make the ultimate sacrifice for my religion, to become a martyr, in the name of Allah,' was his instant reply.

'Come on Mohammed, how religious are these men? If they felt the same way as you, they would step forward, they do not, and will not,' said Rory.

'Maybe, but it is Allah who will reward me, not them, and if they are asking for other reasons, and are just using me as you say, Allah will see that, and they will have to answer to him,' said Mohammed, with a sad smile.

'Can you really be sure, especially if you kill innocent people, some of whom could well be Muslim?' said Maria.

'You are making devices too, these may kill innocent people?' was Mohammed's reply.

'But we are not going to commit suicide, we can walk away, if we don't consider the cause just,' said Maria.

'You are right Mohammed we are being used, it is true, but your people helped us, when we had nowhere to go. We do owe them. My position in Ireland was, in a lot of ways similar to yours in Palestine, and we have suffered at the hands of people in power,' said Rory.

'You may say with some justification, that our religious

141

fervour, is not at the same level as yours,' added Rory. 'However, we have been falsely accused of criminal acts, we have lost people we love to violence, committed by those people, and forced to go on the run like you, we have tried to plead our innocence, but no one is willing to listen. At present, we are looking for revenge, to hit back at a cruel system, and that is against our Christian teaching. We are on a vicious treadmill, if we could get off, we would.'

'I am motivated by a strong religion, I want to embrace it, and answer the call of Allah. I can see your pain, you are good people. I do understand where you are. All I can do though, is to pray to Allah for you, to get him to show you the path to enlightenment.'

'Oh, Mohammed we thank you for your prayers, and we know you will make them. It's just that we feel by remaining alive you can serve Allah better, by spreading his word, you are a kind, loving person, and God knows we don't have enough of them in the world at present, please reconsider,' said Maria.

'Do you know what the timers I make will be used with,' asked Rory, 'and what they will trigger and what the targets will be Mohammed? And there are some technical questions I will want answers to, such as what electrical output and supply is needed?'

'I can't answer any of those questions Rory, sorry, I just don't know.'

'I suppose I will have to ask Roderick,' said Rory.

Roderick was contacted and told Rory he would have to wait for an answer, to which Rory replied that he was unable to start till he had this basic information.

'I want to know, what is going on, the type of device and the strategy they are employing, so I can advise them on the correct timer, for the type of device they wish to deploy,' said Rory.

'They may not tell me, they are very careful about what they are willing to disclose,' was Roderick's reply.

'Roderick I am fascinated how you got involved. I was living in my particular war, you aren't an Arab, why are you living on the edge for them?' asked Maria.

'I am passionate about the Palestinian people,' replied Roderick, 'and the injustices they face in their country, or what, they would like to be their country. They have become slaves to the Israelis. I am doing my bit for their cause, and, I am being paid well for my services, and, that money will get me through college, when all this is over.'

A couple of days later Roderick contacts Rory and tells him that commercial detonators will be used to trigger military explosive. He then informs him that another student, an Arab called Habib, who is studying electronic engineering will contact him in the next few days.

'This Habib, will be helping you, and learning from you. The group are looking to the future, they see him as the next generation of bomb maker. You will like Habib, he is very nice, he is very intelligent, and is a true Palestinian. His whole family was wiped out by Israeli jets,' said Roderick.

'Poor man, we understand what he must feel, I take it he knows what he is being expected to make?' said Rory.

'Yes, I have briefed him. You should talk to him, he may know more. He tells me, that he, like me, has no direct contact with the group, but I do wonder if that is true, he is after all an Arab,' said Roderick.

Before he goes to see Rory and Maria, Habib contacts Michael, to ask him what he should do.

'Go, find out as much as you can about this mystery bomb maker,' said Michael. 'Do not worry, we will cover your back. We'll give you a calculator to carry with you. It has a listening device inside, but, it will also work normally, as a calculator.'

'This man could work out the listening device, and that would put me in a lot of trouble,' said Habib.

'Just leave it there, Habib, abandon it. If he finds it, and works out what is inside, he will not know, which student has brought it there. It is a reasonable object to have as a student. Trust me they will never discover its purpose, after all there would be no reason, just to examine the circuit board of a standard calculator.'

'Look Michael, I am getting very nervous about all this, I am not a natural spy. I dread to think, what this group would put me through, if they ever found out what I have done. I am an Arab, they would see me as a traitor and killing me, would be the last thing I would fear from them.'

'Habib you are a good person, you can see, what they intend to do to innocent people in London, and what they have done all over the Middle East. We have no intention of abandoning you, and, you must tell us, if you sense there is danger to your person.'

'Michael, I feel that danger now, and if they find out, they will want revenge, and they could bide their time, before they act, they are bound to find me. I am grateful to you, for what you have done, but this pressure is getting to me.'

'They will never know the role you are playing, Habib, we will take every precaution to protect you. You are just too valuable to us, you must realise that,' said Michael.

A nervous Habib goes to the address supplied by Roderick and meets Rory and Maria. After cautious introductions, Rory and Habib get down to technicalities. Habib tells them that the group appear to have access to commercial detonators, and military explosive, and adds that before they used homemade explosive. He says that it was very dangerous, nasty stuff, so he is glad they are dealing with more reliable products.

'That makes sense' said Rory, 'that is what they'll give to our suicide volunteer, do you know, if he is going to use a vest or will it be a car, and, do you know why they want extra-long delay timers?'

Habib looks genuinely shocked, 'they never said to me anything about a suicide device, who is this suicide volunteer, I can't see either of you volunteering?'

'He is a Palestinian lad, Mohammed,' said Rory.

'He is a nice boy, and we are not happy about the whole idea. He is just being used,' said Maria.

'Why are you doing all this if you have reservations?' asked Habib.

'We are between a rock and a hard place Habib, and at this point in time, we have little option. Do you know, any more about these long delay timers they are asking us to make? Why do they want, such long delays?'

'Roderick does not know for sure, but he thinks they are to be placed at a student demonstration, his friends, other students, are setting up,' said Habib.

'What do you think, I don't place much reliance, on Roderick, as he is just being used as a gofer?' said Maria.

'I don't trust him, one little bit. I suspect he is in it just for money,' said Habib.

'Do you think, they will place the devices at the venue, days before the event?' asked Rory.

'It could be, if so it will give them time to get out of the country, before the bombs go off,' said Maria.

'They want a large number, some with delays of a few days and some for over a week, any ideas about that?' said Rory.

'I think they plan, to have them go off, at similar demonstrations, on the mainland of Europe,' said Habib.

'So, could be this be part of a spectacular, with devices coordinated to go off all at the same time, all over Europe, what do you think? That would show the world, they have instant support globally' mused Rory.

'I don't know, what to think anymore, are you worried too?' asked Habib.

'Well yes, if they place devices at a demonstration, the only people to get hurt will be the students and activists, who are sympathetic to their cause, which at best is cynical,' said Rory.

'What will they expect to gain?' asked Maria.

'If pro Palestinians are killed, the blame will be put on Israel,' said Habib.

'But they are sacrificing their friends, I am not happy

with being a part of this,' said Rory.

'It is clear the people behind this are risking nothing, and to what end?' asked Maria.

'So they can get greater political influence, for themselves,' suggested Rory.

'I have been thinking the same for some time now, but we should be careful what we say, because all the players in this drama, would sell us down the river, if they faced a problem. I just don't feel that killing innocent people, takes any cause further, except to condemnation, and, we have to live with ourselves afterwards. I am so glad you think this way too,' said Habib with sincerity.

'It is clear why they want such long delays for the devices, and why they want us to test them so accurately,' said Rory.

'The more I hear of this, the less I like it,' said Maria.

'They will be out of the country, when it all kicks off and so should we. And, Habib I think you should be too, we cannot trust them, not to turn on us,' said Rory.

'I am tempted, to rig them so they don't work, and also to add something that makes them easier to find, once they are placed,' suggested Habib.

'We could run Habib, but you would be stuck here at their mercy, unless you ran with us,' suggested Rory.

'I am so fed up, with having to run, because bad men do bad things,' said Maria.

'We would not be blamed, if the Police found the devices, before the activation time, and if we added a transmitter to each timer running off the same power source, they could be guided to them' suggested Habib.

'That means we would have to talk the Police, which would be difficult under the circumstances,' said Rory.

'They would have a receiver, on the same frequency, all the information could be fed anonymously, or through a third party, say someone at the university,' said Habib with his heart in his mouth. He could not help but look to the calculator. 'You are vulnerable to arrest I have no doubt, but now I am not, and could take that risk' said Habib.

'Would you be able to convince the authorities that the threat to the public was genuine? I suppose if the information was really detailed, they would not ignore it. You must not include us in this plan Habib, we will help you, but we do not want any direct contact, with any of the authorities. We have seen enough of unsolicited violence, where only the innocent get hurt, to want to help you, but, we are, as you said, vulnerable. You must realise we are placing a great deal of trust in you' said Rory.

'I am sure, I can do that, and there is no reason to mention you. The thought of having long delayed devices, just ticking away here, will concentrate their minds, I assure you. I think these Arabs trust your skills as an electronic engineer, I see my role as an Arab, is to see you are genuine, and to keep you to your job description' said Habib.

'That makes sense. We can then sort the timed devices out, but what about Mohammed,' asked Maria.

'We can't tell him how we feel, he sounds too much like a zealot,' said Habib, 'and whatever we do, we must keep any plans of that sort away from Roderick, he is an idiot and far too easily bought.'

148

'Yes, he would go straight back to the group,' said Maria. 'I'm sure that if the group do find out, we are in big trouble, or if Roderick is arrested, I believe he is actually wanted, we will be in trouble too. We have to be very careful,' said Rory.

'Habib will you protect us, I know it a big ask, as you don't really know us?' said Maria.

'Yes, I feel I can trust you, and I do have some friends, who may help us,' said Habib. 'They may be able to sort things out, in the long term too. I don't want them involved, unless they are willing, and only then in an emergency.'

'Who are they' asked Rory.

'They are friends at the university, not students, responsible people who have influence, can I leave it at that now?' said Habib.

'Do you know where the explosive is Habib?' asked Rory.

'No, and I don't think Roderick does either, I can't see the group trusting him to any degree, they appear to be very security conscious.'

'What's going to happen with Mohammed?' asked Maria.

'Sadly he is on his own, we have tried to make him see it's a group of criminals, working under the name of Allah, and that they are just using him,' said Rory.

'We have tried,' said Maria, 'he just can't see it, or rather, he just does not want to.'

'What do we do in the short-term, Habib?' asked Rory.

'We can only carry on, so Roderick and Mohammed,

don't get wind of our change of heart. When you have made the timers, and rigged them, I will say I have to have them independently tested, with equipment at the University,' said Habib.

'We have been here, before Habib. We will keep our passports handy,' said Maria with a touch of sadness and concern in her voice.

'Will you trust me, I think I can provide some insurance,' said Habib. 'We must keep in touch.'

'Ssssh I heard someone come in. Hello! It's Mohammed. Mohammed come here. Meet our friend Habib, he is a born Palestinian.'

'Marhaban, kaifa haloka, Mohammed.'

The two conversed for a while in Arabic, before Habib tells Rory and Maria that they have exchanged their stories. It transpires Mohammed was falsely accused of killing an Israeli fighter pilot, which is a sick coincidence, as Habib's family was wiped out by an Israeli pilot.

'Mohammed knows what he has to do, but not when or where, he wants to do this thing, in the name of Allah, so as to glorify his name,' said Habib.

'When they want me, they have to tell me, so I can prepare, I must bathe and be dressed well, before I meet Allah,' said Mohammed.

'Mohammed is there no other way, I do so fear, you are being used,' said Maria with emotion.

'I know you are sad for me, and I understand, it is out of love for me, you say these things, but it is Allah's will, and I feel as though I am blessed, to be the one to serve him.'

'Mohammed, please keep an open mind,' said Maria.

150

'I will my friends.'

Habib then shook hands and embraced Mohammed before he left them. He glanced to see that the calculator was still there and secretly wondered what Michael would make of the conversations, and it was not long before Michael rang him.

'Well that is a turn of events, do you trust them Habib?'

'Yes I do, in spite of not knowing them, till now, I feel they are genuinely fed up with being on the run and being used,' said Habib. 'This is not their struggle, they realise they are paying far too high a price, for the help they got from the group, or, rather from Mohammed, about whom they are genuinely concerned. They do not want to be involved in killing, innocent people, here in London.'

'Are you confident this Rory, will adapt the timers as you suggested, so they are non-functional?' asked Michael.

'Yes, he knows I can test the timers at the University,' said Habib. 'What do you think about adding micro transmitters to the boards, they are small enough not to arouse the suspicion, of anyone not familiar with electronics? It will enable police, or anyone else to find them easily, when placed.'

'Yes, we really like the idea, and we have sourced just such an item, and have them on order, they will be here in forty-eight hours. Will he let them be added?' asked Michael.

'Yes he'll put them into the circuit, and you can check them. You will need a receiver of course,' said Habib. 'Their prime concern, is that they are harmless and found by someone else, before they function, so their hands are not covered with the blood of innocent students.'

'Do you think Roderick knows where the explosive is,' asked Michael.

'I am sure he doesn't,' said Habib.

'Don't push him, I am sure your new friends are right, he can't be trusted by anyone,' said Michael.

'They are worried for Mohammed, he tells them over and over, he is doing this for Allah,' said Habib.

'It is sad, but all these lads who become suicide bombers, are being conned. The main thing, from our point of view, is we know who he is, and that he is the only one, to have got out of Spain. What we don't know, is who is here from the 'Fist of Islam,' and where they are based. It is getting crucial, that we find answers to those questions, and stop this nightmare,' said Michael.

Chapter 7

كل مشكلة لها حل

Every problem has a solution.

In the office of the Bomb Data Centre at New Scotland Yard, the phone rang as Fred Adams entered his office at 8am.

'Hello Fred, this is Helen, Helen Sharon from Jerusalem. How are you? I wanted to get you, while your office is quiet, I know it gets hectic, after 9am your time. Can we go onto a secure line?'

'Yes, this sounds serious, switching now, lovely to hear your voice Helen, all is well here, busy but good. This is an unexpected honour.'

'Fred we both may have a problem. A drug dealer was arrested recently in Tel Aviv, and to cut a long story short, we cut a deal with him for information. He said that we missed a cargo, that should have been of interest to us. He said it was made up of ceramics, and art works, in the form of metal sculptures. The person behind the shipment, is an arms dealer, with connections to a number of Islamic terror groups, and he is not an art lover. What will be of interest to you, is the final destination of the shipment, which is London. My office is arranging for me, to come and see you, I thought I would warn you.'

'Not a warning, Helen, you know you are always welcome. I link ceramics to explosives. Have you any more clues, about these ceramics, what do they look like, and the style of the sculptures. What route is the shipment going to take, and by which form of transport?' asked Fred.

'We have another source, who has given us some more, but that source needs to be protected, which is why I want to come and see you, in person. He thinks the route the shipment has taken, is through Rotterdam, by sea. There are two sealed crates, marked as ceramics from Tel Aviv, the manifest says, they have been produced at the Beersheba Pottery Works, Israel, bloody cheek.'

'Do you know the ship'? asked Fred.

'Yes, it's the M.V. Blue Lagoon, owned by the Blue Funnel Line, and it is a British registered vessel, Fred.'

'I can start making enquiries to track its progress so far, and hopefully, will have an answer for you when you get here. I presume this is between the two of us, at this moment, Helen?'

'Yes please Fred, my boss has just phoned yours, and has got the ok for a liaison visit, so it's official. If you can please keep this from your SB, as long as you can, I would appreciate it, as you know they don't like us.'

'Oh Helen, I can't believe that, on second thoughts I

can, but that is their loss. I take it you will stay at the Embassy. Can you give me your flight details, and we will meet you.'

'Fred, I am about to leave the office now. I will arrive at Heathrow at 6pm on the El Al flight. I look forward to seeing you, and we have much to discuss.'

'Helen, I am counting the hours.'

The Blue Funnel Line had offices in the City of London, and Fred found details of a shipment of pottery from the Beersheba Pottery Works. It had gone as the informant had said, to Rotterdam, where it was transferred onto another of their vessels, and had been taken to Felixstowe, where it was collected by a transport company they use regularly, only two days previous.

The address where the crate was taken to, was a 'lockup' facility in Hornsey, in North London. The particular unit within the facility the goods had been off loaded at, had just been hired by a Mr John Smith, who just signed for the cage where the goods were to be stored, and paid a deposit. The transport company faxed a delivery note, which showed that the crates contained ornamental ceramic plates, and abstract metal sculptures. The cargo had been cleared by customs, and a note was attached to the crates.

In the afternoon, Fred went to the 'lockup' and spoke to the caretaker. He introduced himself as from New Scotland Yard, and that he had information that a large consignment of drugs had been delivered to their facility, recently. It was fortunate, that Fred had been a CID officer at Hornsey, and he knew the facility well, and trusted them to be discreet. He asked the caretaker if he could see all the cages. In one cage he saw the crates from Tel Aviv, and was surprised how big they were, it was obvious anyone moving them would need a lorry and the forklift, at the facility to even move them.

He told the caretaker that he wanted to speak to his boss, who was, fortunately, in the office at the time. The Manager of the facility, was also the owner, and he remembered Fred's face from the past. He said he would be only too willing to phone him, if anyone came to collect the crates, and would delay the process until police came. He said he would keep quiet about Fred's visit, and told the caretaker to do likewise. Fred took a couple of photos of the crates and their markings. The facility closed at 4pm, and would not be open the following day, as it was Sunday, so there would be no movement of the consignment, which was very fortunate.

Fred asked the manager if he would come and unlock the facility for them the following day. The manager said that would not be a problem, and he would stay with them on site, till they had finished what they wanted to do. He pointed out that the cage was locked by Mr Smith, with a padlock supplied by him, and he did not have the key, but he doubted if that would be a problem.

Fred thanked them both for their help, and said he almost certainly would ring the manager on the Sunday, and give a time of arrival. He added that he would be discreet, and no actual action would take place on his premises. The manager had faced similar problems before, and said he knew the drill.

Fred just made the airport, as the El Al jet landed. He waited for Helen at the gate and spotted her amongst the other passengers, as they streamed out onto the concourse. Helen Sharon who worked in the Israeli Bomb Data Centre, was a slim, raven headed girl with piercing blue eyes and a slightly hooked nose. Openly described as a police officer, to all who asked, she was in effect a member of Mossad. She strode purposely through the crowd directly to Fred, without a glance about her.

'Helen, Shalom Aleichem, I hope you had a good journey?'

'Shalom, Fred, well I got here. I sat next to a fat Rabbi, who took half my seat, and muttered prayers to himself, the whole journey, and ate pistachio nuts nonstop, covering me with shells, apart from that ok, how are things with you?'

'I have been busy on your account, and there have been developments, all good, but I will tell you about them in the car,' said Fred.

She gave him a quick hug, and a peck on the cheek.

'I had hoped, you would as you say, get the ball rolling for me. Arek sends his regards, and asks that you keep me in check, as Israel has good relations with Britain at the moment,' she said.

Fred chuckled 'Arek knows, it's impossible.'

Keeping a straight face she replied, 'I know.'

On the journey to the Embassy, Fred briefed Helen on his enquiries so far.

'Tomorrow is Sunday, and the lock-up will be closed, I have the Managers number, and he will unlock for us. We have a chap, who will open the padlock, and lock it again, and an exhibits officer Paul, who you know. He is coming with us. John Smith is unlikely to disturb us. This will give us the perfect opportunity to see those plates, and ascertain if they really are ceramic.'

'I think we both know, what they are going to be, and my money is with explosives. Do we know who this John Smith, really is?' asked Helen.

'We think it is Roderick O'Neill, who is on the run, following a pro-Palestinian demonstration here in London. That was the demo, where Hussein Mustafa was shot. This Roderick is an associate of other students who were arrested at the time. They were released after their well to do parents, mounted legal challenges against their arrest,' said Fred. 'The only evidence against them, for the shooting, was that the gunman came back to the house they were staying in, but, it could not be proved that they were there, when the gunman was. However, there was evidence the gunman was in Roderick's flat, and he has gone on the run.'

'You have not found him yet?' asked Helen.

'No, and I don't think SB have any idea where he is either,' said Fred with a shrug.

'So, Fred the plan is to look inside these crates tomorrow, am I invited?'

'Of course Helen, you might even recognise the pattern on the plates.'

'One thing I can say now, is, there is no Beersheba Pottery Company, and I bet you would not want to eat off those plates, or put anything hot on them.'

'I agree,' said Fred. 'It is unlikely, but if they are drugs, we can pass it on to a friend in the drugs squad. Who is the arms dealer you mentioned, am I likely to have heard of him?'

'Possibly, it is Gregor Gregorov,' suggested Helen.

'Oh yes, he is a slippery individual, and a total 'Walter Mitty,' said Fred. 'I don't think he would know the truth if it bit him, he just tells lie after lie, after lie, and just makes it all up, as he goes along.'

'That is him, he says he was asked to move the crate for this Arab friend, he does business with regularly. He is a Saudi Prince, you know,' said Helen mockingly, in an affected accent. 'Who told him the crate was full of precious works of art! Helen, he said, this beautiful woman, she was the go-between, how could I refuse her. It always is a beautiful woman you know! And, he was to be paid in gold. By the way, he told me, in strictest confidence, it could be missile parts for the Saudi Government, as he does a great deal of work for their Ministry of Defence, as he is respectable, and at the top of his trade. He told me he is only too willing to help my government, but our relationship must be kept a strict secret. He has to be protected, if the Saudi's found out he had been talking to us, they would kill him. He is impossible. I told him, they would have to join the queue behind me. It was only after a few hours of interrogation, that he said the works of art looked to him, to be painted plates, and he could not understand why they were sending lots of plates, that were tourist 'tat,' all round the world, that I started to take him seriously. He was arrested with a load of AKs that he could not account

159

for, by the way.'

'That's our Gregor,' chuckled Fred.

'I hate interviewing him, even when he has been arrested, he makes a pass at me, and, he sweats all the time and stinks. He will not stop talking rubbish, and is in a ridiculous, totally invented, fantasy world. After a few minutes I have a raging headache, maybe that is part of his anti-interrogation technique, who knows?' said Helen, clearly irritated. 'He rarely tells us anything of worth, but this time, it was corroborated by another source, a Palestinian, who was later found in a culvert, with a bullet in his head.'

'Oh dear,' said Fred.

At the Embassy Helen and Fred were met by Michael Hertzog.

'I take it Helen, you have met Fred before?' said Michael.

'We do the same job, he in London, me in Jerusalem, we have been pals for years, but our love affair is, sadly, mostly on the phone,' she said. 'Though, we did meet at the Anti-Terrorist Conference a couple of years ago, and Fred came to Israel to help us with the 'large vehicle bomb question.' He is a friend of Arek too. Yes, the answer to your question is, we are old friends.'

'Well Fred and I know each other well too, he always has a coffee for us at the Yard or a beer in the Albert pub. I am glad Fred you are here now, as I have a warning for you. Your Special Branch are not happy about Helen's visit, and we have concerns about them,' said Michael.

'It's none of their business, they know we are just geeks, we just discuss technology not politics, we have never strayed into their territory. Besides, my boss has confirmed this is an official visit, so what is the matter with them?' said Fred.

'Actually, it is only one man who is the problem. I think you can guess who it is. Please be careful and keep anything you do, and find, close to your chest. If there is a problem let me know, and if I hear anything, I will forewarn you. Of course, I am not saying keep it from your commander,' said Michael.

'Would not dare Michael. I take it the problem's name is Jones. He is the head of the Middle East desk at SB, Helen,' said Fred.

'It's, not that he pokes his nose into everything, he talks to, far too many people Fred, and they have no love for Israel. I can't say any more than that, yet,' said Michael.

'Well we start work tomorrow, Helen will tell you where we are at present. We are going to North London to look at crates of pottery from Beersheba. Tomorrow is Sunday, and SB do not play on Sundays, so there won't be a problem from that quarter,' said Fred.

'That is good, so you have some positive developments already?' asked Michael.

'Yes Helen will tell you. Hopefully, we should at least be able to ascertain if there is a problem, and its magnitude. It is an early start, Helen. I'll pick you up from here. There is only our Exhibits Officer, and one of our locksmiths coming out to play, and they will meet us on the plot, with the lock-up's manager.'

'I take it, he is not involved?' asked Michael.

'No and he has been of help to Police in the past, and at

the moment he thinks we are looking for drugs. He will keep his counsel, as to talk to the 'fuzz' too often, is bad for business. I expect you have plenty to talk about, so I will leave you in peace,' said Fred. 'Helen, don't let him pour too many glasses of wine for you, I don't want you with a hangover, well, not early in the morning anyway.'

'Sweet dreams, Fred,' and she blew him a kiss.

Sunday morning was grey, cold and with drizzle in the air. Fred went to the Embassy, collected Helen, and took her to a little café under the railway arches in Hornsey, where they met the others. The locksmith, employed by the police, had a little van, with his tools, and had Paul the Exhibits Officer with him too. While they had their coffee, Paul was telling Helen about a holiday he had in Eilat, when the manager of the lock-up rang to say he had opened the facility and no one else was about.

They drove into the yard, where the manager was waiting for them. He let them drive their vehicles under cover, and said he would stay in the office, and in the unlikely event of anyone coming, he said he would phone them and stall, whoever it was.

The locksmith had the padlock open in seconds. Paul took photos of the crates, from every angle, incorporating all the markings before they eased off the lid of the first crate. Inside was straw covering hundreds of small plates. They were painted in vibrant colours, with a thick bright lacquer. The designs were typically Arabic, and they gave the impression of being a 'tourist ware' that could be found in any souvenir shop, anywhere in the Middle East.

One of the plates was broken revealing a rough texture

similar to a coarse earthenware.

'Yes, this is explosive, I have even seen these designs before. Fred I sent you photos of similar ones?' said Helen.

'Yes, this lot is likely to be Russian TNT, do you agree? I think we have a serious problem on our hands. Thank God we have this lot under control. Little does our poor manager know, what he has on his facility, if this lot blew he would have no facility.'

'Yes I agree Fred, but where do we go from here?'

'Well there are so many plates, they won't miss one, I will bag it, and get it down to the Fort a.s.a.p. The Fort is the name we give to our explosives lab Helen. Hopefully, they will tell us what we have.' said Paul.

They looked through the crate as far as they could without disturbing it too much and only found plates. A section of the lid held a convenient void and they were able to insert a tracking device. The locksmith who came with them was from the serious crime unit, and his van contained all manner of surveillance and tracking devices.

The actual crate was covered all over with markings, which Helen looked at carefully.

'Paul, I would like to send the photos of the markings to Jerusalem, there are some old marks in Arabic, that indicate to me that at some time, it was in the Lebanon, this could open up for us a line of enquiry, to trace the source of this stuff,' said Helen.

'Yes, I'll have them developed as soon as photographic boys get in tomorrow,' said Paul.

'One mark is of the maker of the crate, and that shows it's clearly Arab,' said Helen.

They proceeded to the second crate which contained the metal abstract art works, consisting of many slim tubes, linked to a thicker tube, attached to a base, with a wire and plug coming from it.

'Helen, I would love to see if there is anything inside these tubes, they are the perfect size to take detonators. The ends are glass with LEDs at the ends, and the tubes, look to be chromium plated aluminium' said Fred.

'Some sort of lighting system?' suggested Paul. 'Shame they are welded together, but I think the main tube unscrews.'

'Here, this one is loose, I think customs, or one of them must have opened it up,' pointed out Helen.

Paul, suitably gloved unscrewed the tube further to reveal a small circuit board and from that went red and white wires that looked a little stiff, and some thinner gauge wires which were orange and blue.

'It does look like a junction for all the tubes, I expect if we plugged them in the lights, would go on and off, change colour or do something in a display,' said Paul.

'Could be Paul, and I bet the thinner orange and blue wires work the LEDs and those thicker red and white wires, look to be single strand copper, and I bet they are detonator wires,' said Fred.

'The red and white wires, are the right type for the detonators, the 'Fist of Islam' got from Libya and currently use,' said Helen.

'The copper commercial ones?' asked Fred.

'Yes Fred, I don't think they would risk shipping their improvised ones, as they are too unstable,' added Helen.

164

'This is serious, we had better put a tracker in this second crate too. Helen, I will have to tell the boss, what we have found. He will than, have to decide whether to sit on these, or take them out of circulation,' said Fred.

'Fred, we have to convince him, to let this lot stay, so we can see who comes for the crates, and then track them, this is a golden opportunity to find out who is behind all this,' said Helen.

'I will ring him, get instructions, and see what he wants us to do now,' said Fred. 'The facility opens tomorrow, and we don't know when this Smith will come to collect the crates, one good thing is, he will have to use a forklift to move the stuff.

'Of course Fred, I will have to tell Michael. I don't know how you can do this, but can you ask your boss, not to confide in Special Branch, Michael is convinced there is an informant in the Branch, talking to someone close to the group.'

'Has he any idea who? And is there is any evidence, Helen? The boss is bound to ask.'

'I don't know Fred, I am as much in the dark as you.'

Paul laughed 'I see when it comes down to it, we are all mushrooms, kept in the dark and fed on, you know what.'

They duly locked up, and thanked the Manager. They said the crates carried contraband, and could he let them know if and when anyone came to collect them.

'I am pretty sure the boss will want someone watching the crates at the very least,' said Fred.

He duly phoned his boss, Commander Parry, and told him what they had found. He agreed the crates had to be watched, and he would get a team together. Fred also told him, that the Israelis had found out the group was getting information from someone in SB, and they asked if the job could be kept strictly in house.

'Right Fred, I will task DI Deaney, Hubbard, and Driscoll. I will hold off with SB for now, but I won't be able to for long. Come back to the Yard now and bring Miss Sharon with you.'

'Yes boss on our way, the Manager is locking the facility now, as we speak. It is not open on Sundays, but will be open from 8am Monday.' Fred explained to Helen that the team the boss was getting together were all, old style CID officers, and no lovers of SB, and once primed, would keep their counsel.

The group duly assembled in Commander Parry's office. DI Deaney a dour Scot said, 'What are you up to now Fred?' as they entered. 'Hello, Helen we met when you were over last, now, this is all getting interesting, very cloak and dagger. The boss will be here shortly, what is in the bag Paul, have you been to that Greek restaurant again?'

'No, and it may not be just a broken plate, if it is what we think it is, it would not be advisable to throw it any-where, let alone on the floor in front of you!' said Paul.

'Is this an Arab job? It's very like the pictures of disguised explosive Fred showed us once,' said Deaney.

'So you weren't asleep during the talk, I'm impressed,' said Fred with a straight face that hid a smile.

'Never miss a second of your talks Fred, I just have to rest my eyes now and again, so I can concentrate more.'

At that moment Commander Parry walked in. He was

an ex-Guards officer, tall grey haired, and immaculate. He had spent most of his police career in the Flying Squad, dealing with organised crime, and was very down to earth, and did not suffer fools gladly, however, he could be a skilled diplomat, when the occasion demanded. He was respected by the troops on the ground as well as his peers.

'Shalom Officer Sharon, so lovely to see you again. I understand you may have uncovered a cache of explosives here in North London?'

'Well it does look like it,' said Helen 'The explosives are disguised as plates and we have seen very similar ones, in a find of arms and explosives in Gaza, just recently. I am pretty sure the actual plate, under the paint is explosive, probably TNT.'

'I have seen this type of plate in one of Fred's reports' added the commander.

'If you look at the break, it is the weirdest form of earthenware, I have ever seen. We know that groups like the 'Fist of Islam' have used this method of disguise, to move the stuff around, and a consignment was seized in Rome last year. Paul has a sample Boss, and it's about to go to Linda Thomas at the Fort for confirmation.' said Fred.

'Linda is on standby, when I drop it in, and she has promised to give us a provisional yes or no right away,' added Paul.

'Well done all, now what is the position at the lock-up?' demanded Commander Parry.

'The manager knows we are interested in the crates but thinks the contents are drugs. TNT is stable stuff, so there is no immediate danger, to him or his staff. The caretaker knows we have an interest at the facility, and the Manager is going to brief him. I know the Manager, and the firm, and they will be discreet. Paul has fitted trackers to the crates, and nothing will be moved from the facility, till tomorrow morning anyway. In view of the amount we are dealing with it was time to come to you for a decision, as to whether to seize it, or to follow it. It is there for a reason, and there must be some plan in place, and a terrorist team is either here, already, or coming soon. I know there are obvious dangers for keeping it live, but also dangers if we don't find who is behind it. Sir, if we take it out of circulation, they could just replace it somewhere else, at the moment we are ahead in the game, and have a chance to identify the team' said Fred.

'I agree, Mr Deaney, you will head up the operation on the ground,' said Commander Parry. 'I want those crates watched. Helen do you know what Michael Hertzog is up to at present? No, that is unfair, do not answer that dear. Lads, I do want this kept tight, so don't discuss this in the Squad or with SB is that clear.'

'Crystal clear,' said DI Deaney.

'The Israeli Embassy have been on to the Security Services, and are keen for Helen to work with Fred. They are afraid there may be a leak and emphasise the need for security. Fred, you will carry on your enquiries with Helen, and report direct to me, or DI Deaney. Is that clear Fred?'

'Yes sir.'

'Helen just deal with Fred. If you have any concerns, or anyone tries to pressurise you, come to me directly. My office is always open to you,' said Commander Parry, with a smile.

'Yes sir,' said Helen.

'Now you two rogues,' looking to Driscoll and Hubbard, 'watch those crates like hawks, follow and for Christ's sake don't lose them. Any movement tell Mr Deaney, Fred, or me. Mr Deaney, this will be 'Operation Spider,' I'll brief Denise Starr, the "Dragon," to her friends, to set up an office where she will fly solo. There'll be a dedicated line for you all to use, and she will handle all incoming calls, and run the office. Now, Officer Sharon, I'd appreciate a heads up, if you get anything through your networks, that might affect the situation. The bottom line is, Helen, I don't want this stuff used on my patch.'

'Yes sir,' Helen replied with a quizzical smile.

'Fred, we'll wait for a reply from Linda at the Fort, if it is positive I may have to increase the squad, how about Stannard and Groves, I think they're suitably Neanderthal, is that ok Mr Deaney,' said Commander Parry with a smile.

'Yes I agree with the comment, and seriously Boss that's fine,' replied DI Deaney.

'Well done all of you, keep me posted,' and with that the commander shooed them out of his office.

'A fine mess you have got me into, again, Fred,' said DI Deaney. 'I didn't say to the Boss, but SB have been sniffing around already, wondering why Helen is here, it's that pompous idiot Jones, him with the bow ties. He heads the Arab desk in SB Helen, if he starts on you steer him to me, and I will suitably advise him.'

That evening Helen talked to Michael at the Embassy.

'I was told you wanted me, specifically me, here on this

job. Now come clean why? You must have a reason,' she said.

'As a child you had an Arab friend, a boy, Mohammed Ali,' said Michael.

'Yes, he was arrested in connection with the murder of one of our pilots,' said Helen. 'I presume he is still in custody.'

'No, he was released,' said Michael.

'I am glad, I never believed he had anything to do with the shooting, he was used as a scape goat, I felt sure,' said Helen.

'Well, that's as maybe, but he was then taken in by the PFLP, and from them, he gravitated to the 'Fist of Islam.' He is very religious, as I am sure you will be aware,' added Michael.

'But I cannot see him as a fanatic. He was a shy boy who loved nature he would not have harmed a fly,' said Helen.

'They have got to him,' said Michael.

'I can't believe it,' said Helen.

'We have intelligence he was at a training camp, and has been groomed for a suicide mission,' said Michael, with a shake of the head.

'Oh, no that is a terrible tragedy, so those explosives we found in that lock-up, will definitely be military, so this could all be linked,' said Helen. 'It's the type of explosive they would need for a suicide operation.'

'Yes, from what you say, the man who hired the lock-up is a British student, part of a group, who have been actively working with the 'Fist of Islam,' though they may not know it,' said Michael. 'They certainly do not know, what they are dealing with.'

'Does Fred know about Mohammed, and the suicide element? They have not faced a suicide bomber here in London yet. I feel sure he will have worked out, that the 'Fist of Islam' are driving this operation?' said Helen.

'No, we have not passed on the information about Mohammed yet, there is a leak at Scotland Yard,' warned Michael. 'We cannot confirm anything yet, about the identity of the leak, though we have our suspicions. We do have sensitive intelligence, that Mohammed is here for one reason only, but we are not in a position to share that information yet. The group are covering their tracks well, they are using the students to do the dirty work, so we don't know which members of the group are here, and where there base is yet.'

'If we work with Fred, surely we stand a better chance of getting close, we trust him to be discreet, and I know Arek, who has worked far longer with him than I, trusts him implicitly. Do not forget this is London, not Jerusalem. His commander has set up a team for this operation, all from their CID, and they are keeping everything, that happens, within that group.'

'Yes, we will bring him into the loop, but not now, we have the students bugged and we have one turned as an informant, their group is starting to fragment, and they may well lead us to the main group,' said Michael. 'Another problem is that they have recruited a bomb maker who is Irish. We think he may be of interest to the British for IRA activities, we don't want them changing their focus.'

'I wish now you had not told me this, I hate to deceive

Fred, friends are hard to come by in this business, hard to make, and so easy to lose.'

'The specific job we have for you, is to get close to Mohammed. We know that this Irishman and his Spanish girlfriend are trying to persuade him not to throw his life away. But, at the moment he just wants to sacrifice himself for Allah. We have most things covered, but the one piece of the jigsaw puzzle we don't have, is details of any proposed suicide attack,' said Michael.

'How do you expect me to do that, if it had escaped you, I am an Israeli? Does he know I am Mossad?' she asked impatiently.

'No, and I don't imagine he knows you are even with the Police. You have to see him as a childhood friend, and I feel, he will reciprocate. Do not, obviously, tell him anything about the situation unless he mentions it. Try to draw him out, anything you can glean, will be of help,' said Michael. 'He has a different address from the main student group, finding that out will be of help. Ask him if he sees any of his old friends, from back home. You know what I want, I know it will be difficult, but anything will be of help.'

'And, you expect me to do this while I am working with Fred?'

'Tell Fred we have asked you to do some digging, to find out who is behind all the interest in Palestinian affairs in the universities in London, as part of a European wide enquiry,' suggested Michael.

'Do you seriously believe he would fall for that Michael, I am not sure I want to tell him lies?'

'I don't want him on board yet Helen, we will tell you when,' said Michael curtly.

So it was, with a heavy heart that Helen went to Fred's office the following morning. She had not been there long, before a tall, immaculately dressed man in a three-piece suit and a bow tie came in.

'Good morning young lady, and why do we have the pleasure of your presence in London?'

'A chance to meet old friends, to update Fred, on recent developments with respect to Palestinian improvised devices, and to get some technical details from British commercial firms,' said Helen.

'The mind boggles. Now what were you two doing here on our Sabbath? I understand you two had a day out together, very cosy!'

'I beg your pardon. I don't know you, and don't see why I should discuss anything with you, and I resent what you imply,' said Helen, glaring at the man, who stepped back.

'You may be a guest here young lady, but you will not talk to me like that, or I will just have you thrown out, and on the next flight home,' he said abruptly.

'Officer Sharon, is here on official business, with the full knowledge and permission of the commander,' said Allen, who worked with Fred in the office of the BDC. 'I will get Fred, he is next door.'

'I am Superintendent Jones of Special Branch, I know you are Mossad, I don't trust you, I don't like you, and you will tell me what you are up to, now.'

'This is an official visit Superintendent Jones, please speak to your commander who has been informed of the visit by Officer Sharon and has approved it. You are not entitled to speak to anyone in this office in the manner you have just done, especially not to a guest of the Anti-Terrorist Branch,' said Fred.

'I am not going to be addressed in this manner, you will be back on division before you can blink, if you don't change your attitude. Now, I will say again what are you doing at the moment with Officer Sharon?'

'Nothing that will affect you Superintendent,' said Fred.

'In case it has escaped you I am the Special Branch officer in charge of Middle Eastern affairs, and, I can demand that you brief me in a proper fashion,' said Superintendent Jones.

'This has gone too far, it is time sir that you speak to my commander before one or other of us says something we later regret,' said Fred.

'Oh I will, you can rest assured on that point. Now apart from the obvious, what is this lady, though I hesitate to say lady, doing here?' said Jones with a smirk.

'Get this bastard away from me before I put him in hospital,' said Helen.

'You'll hear more of this,' he said as he left the office.

'He has gone next door to exhibits,' said Allen.

'Let him they don't know anything,' said Fred.

A couple of minutes later one of the exhibits officers came into the BDC.

'What is going on, that prat Jones came to see us, he was in a right paddy, wanted to know where you were yesterday, and he wanted to see any relevant exhibit book.'

'You didn't give it to him?' said Fred.

'No, who do you think we are, that's up to Paul, and he's down the Fort. So, we told him he would have to wait till he was back. In any case he has it with him.'

'Thanks, it's none of his business. He obviously has an agenda. This is a job in which DI Deaney is the SIO and everything has to go through him, and we are instructed not to discuss it,' said Fred.

'Well he won't get any change out of Dave Deaney, there is no love lost there,' chuckled the exhibits officer.

'Sorry for this Helen, sadly this won't be the last we hear of it, he is bound to make trouble. I am left wondering if he is the leak Michael suspects,' said Fred.

Trouble came directly. Fred and Helen were summoned to speak to the commander in his office.

'I have had a certain superintendent in my office, complaining of insubordination, and a threat to his person from Officer Sharon. I expect you both to act with some discretion, you are on a sensitive enough operation as it is. Care to comment, Fred?' asked Commander Parry, as he shuffled papers on his desk.

'He was officious to say the least. He came to see us with one object in mind, to wind us up. He threatened us both, and the insinuations he made with respect to Helen, were at best insulting. He kept on and on, and would not take the hint. We referred him to his commander, and to you, and he still demanded that we brief him fully. He was trying to force us to tell him what was going on,' said Fred.

'He was rude and insulting, to me as a female, he said, he did not trust me, did not like me, and said I was no lady, and was here, for one thing only. There is a limit to what I can tolerate, commander. He was trying to force the information out of me. I would like to think, this is not the attitude, of all the senior officers in your Special Branch. Fred was very diplomatic, but I am afraid when he said those things to me, I snapped. If he is the leak our Embassy suspect, you would think he would be less obvious, unless he is a total idiot,' said a furious Helen.

The commander could not resist a smile. 'You don't expect me to comment on that. Fred I would have expected you to stop this, before there was any escalation.'

'It was unfortunate, I was not in the office when he came in. Allen tried his diplomatic best, to rescue the situation, but Jones, just was not having it. He should not have waded into Helen, in the way he did, as she was not aware of who he was, and after all she is a guest of our branch, not his. I agree with Helen, he could well be the leak, this was too aggressive an assault for a casual enquiry, and who knows he may be under some form of pressure from outside?' said Fred.

'We don't know that Fred, and you can't go round accusing senior SB officers without some concrete evidence, so you are going to have to be careful. I have told him he is to pass all requests for information, through me, and no one else. I have spoken to Commander SB, who will give him words of advice. I must apologise, on behalf of our police service, he should not have said those things to you Helen, I have told him to apologise, but I fear he will not. It is a shame though, that you both reacted,' said Commander Parry.

'Sir, I feel he would have suspected more if we hadn't,' said Fred.

'You may have a point,' said the commander with a smile.

'He went straight round to exhibits after he left us and demanded to see the exhibit book,' said Fred.

'Did they show him?' asked Commander Parry.

'No Sir.'

'Good, if he comes back refer him straight to me, and tell him that is my instruction to you, following his outburst.'

'Yes Sir,' said Fred.

'Helen, he runs the Middle East desk in SB and speaks Arabic, he has many influential friends, who are, of course, above suspicion. Now, one may be of interest to you, he is the oil tycoon Abdullah Ibrahim, who he introduced to me at a social event, he is very charming, has a beautiful wife and he does a lot of work for charities in the Middle East.'

'Yes, I have heard of him, but he lives very much on the edge,' said Helen.

'Helen, of course I would hate to suggest anything,' said Commander Parry.

'I understand sir, I will be discreet.'

There was a knock on the door and Allen entered.

'Sorry to interrupt sir, but I thought you should know directly, Paul has phoned to say, that Linda at the Fort, has confirmed the plate is all TNT with just a painted and lacquered surface. He said he was getting fingerprints, to go to the Fort, and examine the remains. I told Paul of Superintendent Jones visit too. I trust I did the right thing.'

'Yes, Allen well done. I will make sure you do not have any more trouble from Mr Jones. Helen you might ask

Michael Hertzog about this, Abdullah Ibrahim, see what he thinks?'

On return to the office Fred had a call from the Manager of the lock-up.

'I'm sorry, but there is some confusion over the paperwork governing the hiring of the unit. Mr Smith hired the unit and paid the deposit in cash. However another man, an Asian looking man, came today with the key to the padlock, and briefly examined the crates. He said the hiring would be for a maximum of two weeks, and he would be the man collecting the crates. He said he hoped everything was settled up, ready for him to collect them. My caretaker told him, he would have to pay for the actual hiring fee, and that only the deposit had been paid. The man did not have enough cash, and has paid by way of a credit card.'

The manager was thanked and asked for details of the card. Allen was despatched to collect and exhibit the extra paperwork, and the details of the credit card.

'What did this Asian man think he was doing, surely he must realise we could trace him, from a card?' said Helen.

'It could be, that he does not know what is in the crates, and is acting on instruction. In that case he would just be another cut off, employed by the group,' speculated Fred.

When Allen returned he told them that the Asian man was not aware he had to pay a final instalment, and was not best pleased with Mr Smith, who should have taken care of it.

'I can only assume the group, did not want Roderick to be involved any more, but if that was the case, why didn't they give him cash too?' asked Helen.

'It's just possible they gave Roderick enough money for the whole hiring, and he thought the deposit, was the total amount they wanted, or he knew, and just pocketed the left-over cash. You can bet the group would have given him more money, than he would need,' Allen suggested.

'If that is the case, and I think it very likely, I don't fancy Roderick's chances when the group realise what he did, especially if they find out about the use of the credit card,' said Fred.

The card came back to Imit Patel, an Englishman of Pakistani origin who was an employee of 'Middle East Oil Supplies,' a subsidiary company of 'Middle East Oil' a company run by Abdullah Ibrahim. Imit Patel had been arrested in his youth for possession of cannabis, and he was suspected of supplying students at a university. He had been arrested once for supply of drugs, but was acquitted. At his trial he had been represented by a lawyer retained by Middle East Oil. After the court appearance, he was given employment by Middle East Oil Supplies.

The information, had come from the Drugs Squad, who had also recorded that he was an active pro-Palestinian supporter. They also noted that this was not the only case where Middle East Oil had been philanthropic with respect to young Muslim men, who had been led astray, with respect to drugs.

'Well isn't that a coincidence, Ibrahim has come straight into the frame. We had better take a serious look at him and Middle East Oil Supplies. He is obviously recruiting young vulnerable Muslim men, who he has put under an obligation to him,' said Fred.

A call to Jerusalem revealed that Abdullah Ibrahim was not openly associated with any terrorist group, or was suspected of any terrorist act. However he was known to have supplied funds for charities, which were affiliated to the PFLP.

Helen passed on all the information to Michael, whose men checked out the London town house of Ibrahim. The neighbour was a wealthy Jewish banker, who Michael immediately visited and told him that his neighbour was suspected of being a threat to Israel. He asked him if the Embassy could be allowed to mount a surveillance operation from his house. When Michael asked if he had noticed any strange visitors to the address, the banker said that one stuck out immediately. He was a tall well-dressed Englishman, who wore a bow tie, and his visits coincided with Abdullah's absence abroad. The banker and his wife had toyed with the idea of letting his neighbour know of the man's visits to his very attractive wife.

The Mossad surveillance team was in place for only a day, when they photographed Superintendent Jones visiting the house. A copy of the photographs, were sent to DI Deaney at New Scotland Yard anonymously, with the address written on the back. He showed the photos to Commander Parry, who immediately discussed the development with Commander Special Branch. Interestingly Commander SB revealed that Jones had registered Ibrahim's wife as an informant.

Meanwhile Michael managed to arrange a staged meeting between Helen and Mohammed Ali. He had established that Mohammed went for coffee at a particular café every morning. It was there that Helen suddenly appeared and went over to him. At first she had a problem identifying him as his appearance had changed dramatically, he was thin and looked ill. She went and sat at his table and asked if he minded, if she joined him.

'No, please do,' he said with a smile.

Helen ordered a coffee and hesitated, before staring at Mohammed.

'Is it you Mohammed, really you?'

'My name is Mohammed, yes. Do you know me? You do look familiar. Who are you?'

'It's me, Helen, we knew each other many years ago.'

'Oh, Helen, yes, how lovely to see you.'

'I heard you got in trouble. I never believed what they said of you, I did say that to the police at the time. I am so glad it all got sorted out in the end, and you are free. How long have you been in London? Do you live here now?' she asked. 'Please tell me all your news?'

Mohammed looked nervous, 'Helen at the time, I tried to tell them I was not involved, but they wouldn't listen to me. But it has been resolved, and it is in my past, hopefully forgotten.'

He said he loved seeing her again, but he did not wish to be reminded of that time in his life. He said he was just visiting London. She said she would love to spend time with him, and suggested they go for a meal.

He became agitated, and said that would not be possible. He added that he had lost faith with the modern world, and had given his life now to the service of Allah, and was in effect looking more to the next world, than life in this one.

'All the people I really loved have been taken away from me, there is little for me in this world,' said Mohammed, who looked as though he was about to cry.

She told him that this was so sad, that if he felt he needed a shoulder to cry on, she was willing to supply one. It became clear to her that he was not going to tell her where he was staying, or give any hint as to what he was planning, so she gave him the number of her mobile phone, and asked him to call her, and repeated, that she would love to see him again.

When she briefed Michael she said she gained the impression he would be willing to be a suicide bomber, and was showing all the psychological tell-tale signs, that he was about to give himself to Allah that way.

'He has not listened to what Maria and Rory were telling him for sure, and they put up a good argument, and now he won't listen to you. Sadly, it is clear he will not be diverted,' said Michael.

The conference with the PLO and the Israeli's was only a few weeks away. Superintendent Jones became aware that there had been enquiries into Ibrahim's companies, and he tried again to find out what exhibits had submitted to the explosives laboratory. He was unable to get past DI Deaney who proved to be a rugged impenetrable barrier, to all his enquiries. All the documents relevant to 'Operation Spider' were locked away, and Jones was not made aware where the office of 'Operation Spider,' was located. Dr Thomas had also been briefed not to discuss the case with anyone, as there was a security problem.

A fingerprint on the broken plate came back on the Mossad data base to a PFLP member Abu Salem, who was suspected of being the leader of the 'Fist of Islam' group. The information was passed to 'Operation Spider.' There was Speculation as to when the print was made, and it was decided that it must have been when the items were packed. Questions were raised, as to whether Salem was in London now, and as to what he planned to do, or get Mohammed to do for him.

Chapter 8

كل ما هو جميل، الناس يريدون كسره.
أنتِ جميلة، و أنا خائف.

*Anything that is beautiful, people want to break.
You are beautiful, and I'm afraid.*

When Roderick next appeared at Rory's flat, he had a number of boxes in carrier bags.

'These are the containers for the long delay devices,' said Roderick as he dumped them on a table.

'They're too big just for the timers, what else is going in there?' asked Rory.

'The explosive silly,' said Roderick.

'When is that coming, it's bound to be a high explosive charge, to be able to fit into those boxes?' asked Rory.

'Yes, and I don't know when it will come. As soon as I get it, I will bring it to you,' said Roderick. 'Has Habib checked those timers yet? We want each unit assembled ready to go as soon as possible.'

'Not yet,' answered Rory, 'he has to use the oscilloscope at the University to do that, and he has to be careful, so as not to arise any suspicion. He is doing all the work overnight, when no one is around in the lab, and he can't do the work every night, as that would draw attention to him.'

'Well he had better get a move on, they are impatient. Tell him, they want it all done as soon as possible, apparently, time is running out,' said an impatient Roderick.

Rory duly phones Habib, and says the group are impatient. Habib replied that the group will have to wait till the coast is clear, for him to complete the last few, as the university will be suspicious of too many long nights in the lab.

As soon as Roderick had left, Habib phoned Michael for instructions. He tells Michael that he has checked all the timers, and labelled them with the delays the group required. He confirms that no power will go through when the sequence has played out, and that the tiny transmitters, that Rory got from him, have been added, and will operate as soon as the power is switched on to the circuitry.

Michael tells Helen that all is set, and the timed devices are safe. She is still concerned that they are operating without any authority, on foreign soil.

'Michael I don't care what you say, I am going to tell Fred what is going on, this has to be a joint operation. If Fred did this in Israel, what would you say?'

'Fair point, but his bosses will not approve, of some of the things we have done,' warned Michael. 'If we tell him now, and ask him to keep it to himself, which is what I would want, then, when they find out, as they will, he is going to be in real trouble.'

'They have set up a dedicated, safe team, we have to trust them,' said Helen. 'Commander Parry is no fool, he has been alerted with respect to Jones, and surely the risk to our operations is negligible now. The students you have bugged in their homes, can afford good lawyers they will say you acted illegally, and that could well compromise any prosecution, brought by the Anti-Terrorist Branch, or, at the very least make it awkward for them at court. Let me ask you, will you be willing to go to court, as they will insist you do?'

'Helen listen to yourself, we are fighting the 'Fist of Islam' here, you see what they are doing in Israel, if we have any chance of getting at their leadership, we have got to take it, even if that means upsetting a few people on the way.'

'Right, if this all goes ahead, even if there is a result. They will not believe Fred was not in this with me, from the start. The first thing that they will do, is send me back to Israel, and Fred will be removed from his post,' said Helen. 'If his immediate bosses do not take that action, their Special Branch will demand it, and, back home, Arek for one, will crucify you. What does the Ambassador say, I hope he has been informed of all the things you have done?'

'Yes he knows, and he says do what has to be done. If it goes wrong, he says I will be on the first plane back to Israel.'

'Right, Michael you have to speak to the Ambassador again now. If this goes wrong, there will be a diplomatic row like no other before, and you will hand the Palestinians all the ammunition they need. Think about it. I am going to talk it over with Fred, I know he will not panic, and will think of a way, we can get out of this situation, without too much egg on our face.'

'Helen, I can't stop you, but if what you propose goes wrong, we are all in trouble.'

Helen invites Fred to dinner at a quiet restaurant at the back of Victoria Station and duly unburdens herself, briefing him on all the action that Michael has taken.

'No wonder they got you over from Jerusalem, as much a diplomatic mission as an operational one,' said Fred. 'Michael has to talk to the Ambassador now, get him to go through diplomatic channels, back to our government. Stress that all is under control, but a joint effort is essential now, not only from a diplomatic angle, but from a legal standpoint. Tell him to do it now, I cannot sit on this for any length of time. The British public is at risk, and the only thing safeguarding them, is actions taken by an Arab, arrested as a pro-Palestinian activist, and a known IRA terrorist. Look at it from our perspective, this is a seriously dangerous game Michael is playing, not with his people, but with ours. Helen I want to hear from the Ambassador, that this course of action has been set in motion. I want to come to the Embassy now, tell Michael what I said.'

Helen rang Michael and said they were on their way, and what Fred proposed. Michael said that he would relay what Fred had said, but could not guarantee that the

Ambassador would see him, and could well object to having his arm twisted.

At the Embassy, the Ambassador did meet Fred and Helen with Michael in attendance. 'Fred I agree, it is time for this operation to be put on a formal basis. I have spoken to Jerusalem already, and in spite of it being late there, our Foreign Ministry are contacting their counterparts in London. They will be briefed, including our reservation over your Special Branch. I have told them that Mossad have everything under control. I fully understand your fears over the legal position, and the last thing we want, is to make any action taken, more difficult than it already is. Our problem is very much your problem, I fully understand. I agree with Helen's point, you should speak to your boss without delay. I am sure within hours your government will be briefed, so he should be warned in advance, and hopefully that will go some way to pour oil on troubled waters. Fred I will also say that you had no prior knowledge of our operations, and had taken the correct action, once you were alerted.'

'Thank you sir, I had better speak to Commander Parry now.'

Fred rang the commander at home, and passed on what had occurred at the Israeli Embassy, and a brief outline of what the Mossad had been up to. He said that he would sit down with Helen, and draft out a full briefing note for him.

'Very good Fred, I will be in the office at 7am, we have to get on top of this before it gets very messy. Thank Helen for me, the pair of you have been dropped into a very difficult situation. For now, we all have to be calm and keep clear heads.'

The diplomatic wheels were set in motion during the night. COBRA was convened, and decided that MI5 would keep a watching brief over a joint operation, headed by the Commander of the Anti-Terrorist Branch working with the Mossad attached to the Israeli Embassy in London.

At 7am Fred and Helen produced a typed briefing note outlining the operations currently running for the commander's information. Commander Parry thanked them for their prompt action, and Helen for taking him into her confidence. I trust that everything is under control. I expect to be briefed in detail by Mr Hertzog, at his earliest convenience.

Commander Perry was duly informed of the situation by the Commissioner, and told to take the nucleus of his team to the Israeli Embassy for a briefing. He went with DI Deaney, Fred, and Helen. At the embassy, the Ambassador and Michael met them, together with an MI5 agent, who was there to observe.

'Commander I have been very correctly reprimanded by Fred, for not joining with you sooner on these operations, and I am indebted to him, for coming to me directly,' said the Ambassador. 'It demonstrates the level of friendship that exists between our police forces. In Israel we have to face these situations on a daily basis, as we live amongst those, who would challenge our sovereignty, in the most aggressive of ways. This is your home, and you should have control of your destiny, however we faced here some issues of security, as I am sure you will be aware and we were frightened, yes frightened, that the progress we were making to catch these active terrorists, would be undone. Now, we are confident that this issue has been addressed, and we can move forward together. I have done the diplomacy bit, and I will hand you over to Michael Hertzog, who can answer your questions in more detail.'

The commander replied 'I am sure we can move forward. I would like to thank Helen for her part in engineering this rapprochement, it could not have been easy. She has with Fred, already sketched out the situation. I trust Michael can now put flesh on the bones, so that we can form a plan, to cope with this very difficult situation.'

Michael went through the operations in detail. They immediately got down to business and agreed the surveillance on the lock-up should be strengthened. They agreed Dr Thomas should check the timers and circuitry at the university, immediately before Habib released them to Rory for Roderick.

DI Deaney asked, 'what is an Irishman doing here with this team. He has an IRA history, do we really trust him?'

'It's a long story, and he is here with an ETA girl,' said Michael.

'Are there any other surprises?' asked Commander Parry, and he added 'the Guardia Civil in Spain and the RUC in Norther Ireland would love to talk to this pair, especially if Rory was the maker of the timers. We have been trying to identify who made similar ones, for some time now.'

'I understand commander, there may be some unfinished business, however, can that wait for now?' said

Michael. 'Habib has been turned, and basically does anything we want him to, and he is genuinely fed up with all the violence, and conflict, and will do anything to stop it. We have listened to him discuss it with Rory and Maria, and it is obvious from what they, themselves have been saying to each other, in private, that they are of the same mind. They are genuinely horrified, at the thought of taking any part in killing of innocent, but misguided students, at a demonstration, for a cause that they have sympathy with. It was they who formed the plan, to modify the timers and tag them.'

'So what you are saying, once Dr Thomas has cleared them, we can let them be placed, and they will be safe. What will that gain us, why don't we just take them out of circulation?' asked DI Deaney.

'They are safe, the transmitters once active, will allow police to locate them when they are placed,' said Michael. 'We can watch who places them, as we know the target area, and the fixtures the devices are going to be put into. Once your policeman has found one, the bomb squad can defuse it, and the media will carry a story of police vigilance, preventing a major terrorist incident. This, we hope will safeguard our informants, since the failure of the operation would have had nothing to do with them.'

'What use will the informants be after this, do we take them out of circulation?' asked Deaney.

'They may be approached again, by the group to do something else, and in a hurry, it would be essential to know what that was,' said Michael. 'It appears the group want their actions to coincide with the political meeting, so time is an issue for them. We have all of the students they are using, under some form of electronic surveillance, and once there is direct contact with the group, I suggest that they all get put under surveillance. The group have been ultra-careful in their security, and it has been so difficult, to know who is driving them. They use the students, as far as they can, in order to protect the identity of the group members. We suspect it is Abu Salem, from the 'Fist of Islam' who is leading the operations, but we do not know where from, and who is with him, or where he is.'

'What are we doing with the crates in the lock-up? asked Deaney. 'The suicide bomber would want to use this type of explosive in his device?'

'We let the crates be taken, and we will monitor them, see where they go, they obviously do not trust Roderick, with this phase of the operation, so they could be taken to the heart of the groups operation,' said Michael. 'We have the added advantage of course, that the crates have been tagged, as insurance.'

Commander Parry asked, 'What about this Mohammed Ali?'

'That is a problem, Helen knew him as a child, and has seen, and spoken to him. She has noticed a great change in him, he has become a manic depressive, with a religious fixation,' said Michael. 'He does not know who she works for, so she may be able to try again, first to find out more about what is going on, and secondly to make him see reason. Habib, Rory, and Maria have all tried to convince him he is being used, and the group's agenda does not have religion as its number one priority. If we can watch him, we will see signs when he prepares himself for martyrdom. He is determined, it would seem, to give himself to Allah. We do not know how the group is making contact with him, but we are working on that. Habib may be able to find that out, but Habib must not put himself on offer, he is too valuable to us. All we can do is maintain a tail on Mohammed, which at the moment is not too difficult, as he stays in his room and prays for most of the time.'

'What about Jones do we arrest him or let him run. I would be less than honest, if I said I liked the man, he is a prat,' said DI Deaney.

'I feel we should let him run unaware of what we know. I know it is dangerous, and he could cause problems,' said Michael. 'However the priority must be to identify the group. I see Abdullah Ibrahim, as a major line of enquiry and Jones's link to him, or his wife, is a possible way of getting closer. I am afraid Superintendent Jones must be watched very carefully.'

'Boss, how about opening our safe house in Pimlico as a base, it will take us out of the yard, and away from Jones and SB, so we won't have to watch over our shoulders all the time?' suggested DI Deaney, 'And we can get cosy with our friends from Israel too.'

'Yes, Dave, do it,' said the commander and Michael agreed, nodding his head.

'What about Ibrahim's companies, could we get someone in there?' suggested Michael.

'That would be dangerous, most of them are indebted to him in one way or another, like this Patel. We don't know, but it's possible that some employees of the firm, could be members of the group,' said Dave Deaney.

'We have to watch Roderick closely too, they are still using him as a go between, and as the line of communication with the students and Rory,' suggested Fred. 'He may provide us with clues as to when any event will take place, as I am sure any request for the students to do anything, will come through him still' said Fred.

'Yes Fred agreed, he must be a priority,' said Michael and Commander Parry agreed.

'So 'Operation Spider' is spinning a web, in which we hope to ensnare this group. Michael we will have to make use of your surveillance capability, and transfer the electronic monitoring, to our new base, so it can be co-ordinated with the physical surveillance. You will have to have a presence, there twenty-four seven.'

'Yes commander that will be good,' said Michael.

With that the meeting broke up, and the various elements went away to start spinning the web of ensnarement. As they left Commander Parry pulled Michael to one side.

'Michael, if you ever play stunts like that again, on my patch, without my knowledge, I will personally kill and bury you, is that clear. Having said that, if everything works out, I hope, I will be glad you did. You son of a bitch, you must like living dangerously, is all I can say.'

Michael smiled, 'Yes commander at the time, I could see no other way.'

The Mossad team worked furiously overnight, to transfer their operation to the base in Pimlico. They had just set up, when they listened in horror as Roderick related to

Rory how Mohammed had met Helen. He went on to say that the group were furious with him, and had told him that if he met with her again, they would take it out on his sister's children, who were in a camp in the Beqaa Valley.

It was not long before Mohammed, came to see Rory and Maria, he was clearly distressed and after Rory offered him a shoulder to cry on, he collapsed into floods of tears.

'This is a pointless blackmail, they just had to say, don't see her. Why did they have to threaten the children, what have they done? What more do they want from me? I am willing to give my life for Allah. What more can I give?'

'Just go Mohammed run, they could never carry out their threat,' said Maria.

'Oh, yes they could and would, they are that ruthless,' moaned Mohammed.

The police team duly had their first council of war together. Michael said that they were all friends, and that there would be nothing discussed in Hebrew. They agreed that the group, by being heavy handed, had made a tactical error, in which they could have alienated Mohammed. While they discussed which was the best way to exploit the situation, a call came from the surveillance team at the lockup. A van had entered and two men had asked the caretaker to let them collect their two crates.

The caretaker told them they would have to wait for a little while, as the forklift was in use, and invited them to have some tea. Once he had distracted them, he phoned the number he had been given. The delay allowed a strengthened surveillance team to get in place, and get good photographs of the two men and their van. The van bore the logo of 'Middle East Oil Supplies,' and was duly followed to their warehouse complex, where it was just possible to see that the crates were offloaded into an area outside a porta-cabin. The men then removed the plates and sculptures and took them inside the porta-cabin. A little while later three other men entered the building, and were photographed on leaving. Michael at once said he thought that one of the men was Abu Salem.

They agreed that it was likely the explosives would be prepared in the portacabin, and the detonators removed from their tubes there too.

'So will they take the explosive to the group, so they can assemble the devices? Or will they have the timer boxes taken to them at the porta-cabin?' asked Michael.

'The timers and the boxes are at the students flat, they will have to be united, I bet they'll still use Roderick, and he will collect them.'

The following day that is exactly what happened. Roderick was heard to confirm with Rory, that the boxes had power packs, timers, and output terminals. Roderick then took the boxes to the yard of 'Middle East Oil Supplies' and put them in reception in bags, and that, is where he left them.

'They are still being cagey, Roderick went nowhere near the porta-cabin. Now that the boxes are wired up, they'll not need Rory anymore. I expect they have been working on stripping the lacquer and paint off the plates. What do you think Helen? Will they bother to melt down the explosives into little slabs, so they can be fitted in the voids in the boxes?' asked Fred.

'I think they have too,' said Helen. 'They would have broken the plates in bits. The explosive itself will now be in a crumbly form, so they must get it into solid lumps to fit in the void in the boxes.'

'So they will have to make moulds, then melt it, that will take time,' said Fred.

'The moulds may have been prepared already, it should not take too much more time. I have not seen any heating equipment go in, but then it could be there already. I think the pace is hotting up, if you will forgive a pun. Those devices will soon be ready to be deployed,' said Helen.

'What we know for certain is that the time delay is three days. Habib has said they only wanted the three-day timers in these boxes. One presumes the other timers, the really long delay ones, are for use abroad. What we will have to do is notify the ports to search thoroughly any of the vehicles of the company going to mainland Europe, in the next few days. We know they want to have a coordinated attack, they will have the power on, so, the timers will have been activated already, as will the transmitters Rory and Habib put on. We have to ask the customs to use scanners to pick up the transmitter signals when they search, it will save them time and effort, so they will need the frequency details,' said Fred.

DI Deaney agreed and a 'secret memo' went out to all the ports serving mainland Europe.

'Now Fred, does that mean they will place the devices within three days from now?' asked DI Deaney.

'Sorry, it is not as easy as that, the timer's delay will only start when the group switch the power on,' said Fred, 'and it is possible we won't know when that is. However when they give the boxes to the students to place, we will know, that we have a maximum time limit of three days, the students cannot alter or activate the timers themselves, unless they ask Rory or Habib, and we will know if that happens.'

'Right, we know the demonstration is set for the day before the meeting between the PLO and the Israeli delegation, so we have a time frame, for them to place the devices, yes?' asked Dave Deaney.

'We should learn from the students, when Roderick delivers the completed devices to them,' said Michael. 'And we can gear up the surveillance, and response teams accordingly.'

'Yes, the window is getting smaller, but that means they have a plan. They will want to be out of the country when it all kicks off, I bet,' said Helen.

'But that will leave Mohammed to his own devices, I presume he will, or has been briefed on what he has to do?' said Fred.

'He will be well trained on the set up, and activation of the device. He would have been instructed, in the tactics of delivery, at the training camps he attended in Lebanon,' said Helen.

'What we do not know, is what the specific target is, and how he will get close to it. He has a suicide belt, I understand. Now, that will give us problems, if we have to stop him, especially in a public place? Any ideas?' asked Dave Deaney.

'Right, let us try and work this out logically,' said Michael. 'They know the meeting will be well policed, not only by you, but by us as well. They must therefore know, he won't be able to get far enough into where the meeting is being held, to be effective.'

'Aren't the PLO being housed at a hotel the night before the meeting? That is a possible place for the attack, I know there will be security but it is more discrete, so as not to show out,' asked Fred.

'That has been kept secret, I know. The Manager has been briefed to say that wealthy, influential guests are coming to stay, but not who exactly they are. That is, if he is asked. From what I hear they have been no enquiries. But, and it is a big but, SB will know and that means Jones will know, and we cannot rule out that he will not tell Ibrahim's wife. So the cat could soon be out of the bag, if it has not already been let out. There has been no contact by phone between Jones and the Ibrahim's in the last few days, so ok, for now,' said Michael.

'They are bound to keep Mohammed away from the students, and Rory and Maria, especially if they have heard that they have tried to persuade him, not to go through with the attack,' said Fred. 'Now the threats made to him, make more sense.'

'What have we got to do, what are our priorities?' said DI Deaney. 'Keep the meeting safe, keep the delegates safe, intercept Mohammed and defuse him, which could mean shooting him, and grab Abu Salem and any of his group's members that are here, and recover any outstanding weapons, explosives and devices.'

'No problem,' said Michael with a sigh.

'Can't we change the hotel, just before the PLO arrive?'

suggested Helen.

'Yes, there is a contingency plan for just that,' said DI Deaney 'We would not tell the original hotel at all, and the new hotel just before they are due to arrive. They are keeping rooms free, for what they have been told is a 'police seminar group.' Our team, which did not include SB, carried out those arrangements and the 'Diplomatic Group,' will be briefed just before it happens, to actually police the venue.'

As they talked Roderick was summoned to a meet with a group member and was given the completed devices, which he carried, now much heavier to Hilda and Pete's flat.

He told them the devices were set to go off, well before the demonstration, and that they would be in no danger placing them. They would then turn up, after all the bangs, and demonstrate as police were clearing up. This would show the strength of feeling, and the resolve, to stand up for the Palestinian cause, despite what would be seen as an Israeli attempt to cause havoc and injury at the demonstration. If the police tried to block them, the resultant struggle and publicity would have an even greater impact, through the media. He said he thought it was a brilliant plan, a master stroke.

Roderick also said he would help place the devices, they would use a van, work in overalls, and just take off the plates at the base of lamp posts, and slip the boxes into the void, as simple as that, and put the plates back on. He said that there are plenty of lamp posts round Duckett's Common, the blast would take them down, all over the road, and bits would fly onto the grass common.

'If these things go off while the demo is on, dozens of people could be killed or injured,' said Hilda.

'Not, if they go off before,' said Roderick.

'When will that be?' asked Pete.

'At 4am on the dot, when no one is in the square,' said Roderick.

'I want to make sure they will do that, I want to speak to Rory,' said Hilda. 'I don't want the blood of innocent people on my hands, especially those who are working for our cause. I am not sure I trust the group anymore.'

'Can't they just be found, that will have the same impact as if the plan you outline went through,' said Pete.

'The group won't be happy unless they have a bang,' said Roderick.

'Look we want to talk to Rory,' said Hilda, 'before we are prepared to do anything, get Rory here now.'

Rory was contacted and immediately came round to the flat. The concerns were put to him straight away. He explains that since he did not switch the power on, he has no idea when the devices would activate.

'The only person who will know is the group member, who set the circuit live,' he said.

'I am not happy about this,' said Hilda 'we have no real control. I don't want to go ahead.'

Roderick said 'the group will get nasty if you don't. Look, I will go to the phone box, call them, and make sure, exactly, when the bang will occur, hang on, I'll be back shortly.'

As soon as Roderick had cleared the room Hilda asked

'can't we do anything Rory? We do not, want to kill any innocent people, our friends.'

'You should have thought of that, before you started with all this,' said Rory.

'For Christ's sake can't you do anything?' said Pete.

'Don't panic just go with Roderick, nothing is going to happen, and the devices will be found by police before they go off, they will search the area of the demonstration. They always look where you intend to put them, there won't be a problem,' said Rory.

'Can we trust this will happen, Rory, we have to know?' said Hilda.

'Yes, trust me. I can hear him coming back, just go with what he says, it will be alright,' said Rory, anxiously.

Roderick looked annoyed and concerned when he entered the room.

'They are angry, just go ahead or they will come, and make sure you do, and it will be the worse for you,' he said. 'This lot, when they are angry, they get nasty. They say the devices will function at 4am, as arranged.'

'Roderick, relax, it's ok, I have talked to them, and we go ahead as planned,' said Rory.

'Good' said Roderick, 'I'll be round later, to see you and Maria.'

'Yes, I want to know where we stand now that things are coming to a head. We have done our job, and will be of little further use to this group.'

A few hours pass, and Roderick arrives at Rory and Maria's flat. He says that the couple should go, get out of the country back to Spain. The group will stop paying for the flat shortly.

'They have given you good papers, and have paid for your work. I have here a bonus, the final payoff settlement.'

Roderick passed them a brown envelope of cash.

Maria slid the cash out of the envelope, which was not sealed.

'This will get us back to Spain but that's it, I see they are less generous, now we have stopped being of use to them.'

'That's them all over I am afraid, they need money for bombs and guns too,' said Roderick.

'They have some good backers, so I bet they cream a fair amount off for themselves,' said Rory.

'I would not try to squeeze any more out of them, if I was you. Now, I have work to do, to make sure those students set up the diversion, I must go,' said Roderick.

'So that Mohammed can die for them,' said Maria.

'Well, yes, he wants to give himself to Allah, haven't you heard,' said Roderick.

'Roderick, we are the ones taking the risks, doing their work for them, what do you get out of this?'

'Till now they have paid me really well, I shall do a runner soon, when the final payment comes in,' he said.

'It has been one big adventure for you, hasn't it Roderick. Mohammed will kill himself, and I can see them setting you up to take the fall for the rest, and, where will they be? Away abroad somewhere in the Middle East, where they cannot be touched. That is why they are using the long delays. Wise up Roderick, you could be in trouble here,' said Rory.

'So, you reckon I should get my final settlement and run too?' said Roderick.

'Just run Roderick,' said Rory.

Roderick left the flat and headed off to see the group.

'Look this envelope has been opened, I bet Roderick has taken a cut out of the cash already. I am sure they will have seen through him. If he tries to be greedy, or threaten them, I cannot see Roderick lasting too long,' said Maria.

Roderick phoned the group, who told him to meet them at the offices of 'Middle East Supplies,' and they would negotiate his final settlement. He told them that Rory and Maria were not happy with their pay off, and wanted more money. Abu Salem said he was sad to hear that, as he felt he had given them a fair payment, that they had enough money to set themselves up in Spain. Roderick told him, that they had been the ones to take the risks in this operation, and they should be compensated.

'They are so ungrateful,' said Abu Salem, 'I think it is time, we sent you all a message.'

Later a large bundle is carried from the porta-cabin to a member's car and is placed in the boot. The member drives to the reservoirs at Cheshunt and deposits the weighted bundle into a dyke. It is not till two weeks later, that a dog walker finds Roderick's body. He had been shot down through the head. A label with the logo of the 'Fist of Islam' was stuck to the remains of his forehead.

Chapter 9

كر بغيرك

Think of others.

The group phoned Habib, and told him to tell Hilda and Pete to go on and place the devices, and that Roderick would not be joining them. The van with the devices, and their overalls, was outside their flat.

'I don't like the sound of that, where do you think Roderick is?' said Pete.

Habib said calmly, 'place the devices as they said, there should be plenty of time to run on the delay. They won't want them going off in any old street, they want them to have an impact. Well, that is what they hope. If you do that, and the police find them, you cannot be blamed, and they will not come chasing you. I can see no other way out.'

'We are still not happy, but I suppose we have no other choice,' said Hilda.

1am, at Wood Green, Duckett's Common, and it was raining. Pete drove the small blue van slowly around the square, the lights shone across from the bus station, reflecting in the puddles. The Underground sign shone bright, against the black background of the sky.

There was only one person on the green, and he was very drunk, a distorted sound came from his mouth, 'singing in the rain, singing in the rain da, da, da, da, singing in the rain.' These seemed to be the only part of the lyrics he could remember in his befuddled state. He clutched a large plastic bottle of cider in one hand, and took a swig every so often, as he staggered around in a circle.

There were a number of cars parked against the pavement, on the opposite side of the green, from the bus station, and amidst them, in strategic places, were two unmarked vans.

'The rain has kept everyone indoors, and got them hurrying home from the pub, except for Gene Kelly there. Come on, go home you idiot,' said Hilda.

'I think we can take it, that it is all clear. I can't see him remembering a thing in the morning, except that he got wet,' said Pete.

'Still, we had better wait, we can't risk it,' said a nervous Hilda.

'If we pull close to each post, he can't see anything,' said Pete.

Hilda took the wheel, and Pete got the devices ready in a stack in the front of the van. She drove close to each post, so that Pete was shielded from view, except for the large terraced houses, running down the side of the square, away from the bus garage. The front doors and windows were high enough, to make it difficult for anyone to see what the crouched figure was doing. In his overalls, he looked like he was from the electricity department of the council, checking the operation of the lamp posts.

Pete used his screwdriver to open the cover and just slipped in the boxes. They moved slowly and systematically round all the posts, till Pete said 'that was the last one. Let's go, I am soaked.'

'Not as badly as Gene Kelly there, look he is still going. Poor sod, and no one saw his performance, shame,' said a relieved Hilda.

The occupants of the other vans were also aware of the 'cider drinker,' but they were focused on what Pete was doing. They recorded each post, which were numbered, and at one they got a good photo of his face, as he slid the device inside the post. They noticed that he made no real effort to secure the cover plates which would make the bomb disposal man's job, a lot easier. They tested the scanner, and immediately picked up the signals from all of Habib and Rory's modified circuits, with some relief.

As they drove away, the man christened Gene Kelly, by the watchers, danced his way over towards the Underground, and slumped against the wall, under the London Underground sign, and fell asleep.

The 'Operation Spider' surveillance team whispered quietly, to each other.

'Shall we get the local nick to pick him up, before he gets pneumonia'?

'No better not, they will wonder why we are here,' said an observer.

'Where is a policeman, when you want one?'

'The modern generation don't go out in the rain, didn't you know,' was the reply from his colleague.

'So, it's left to us stupid old sods, is it?'

'What do you think? Right, we have a tight schedule let us send this lot back to HQ. You have got all those lamp-post numbers?' said the watcher.

'Yes all logged and mapped, ready for your mate from Hornsey, Fred, all he has to do is go and find them.'

'He has the numbers on the radio, we gave him. He is a good lad and will not let us down. So it's his turn to get wet,' said Fred, the watcher.

2.15am, PC Malcolm Jordan, ex Royal Marine, wandered seemingly without a care in the world, and oblivious of the rain into Duckett's Common. He stopped by the first lamppost, and immediately called Hornsey Police Station, to say he had found a suspect device, and a number of lampposts had been tampered with and other suspect devices were in them. The duty officer attended and the bomb squad were called.

As if by magic, the white bomb squad land rover appeared within ten minutes. Six other policemen were summoned to the scene, and started to set up cordons, and close roads. The bomb disposal man directed, from the observation van, very quickly removed all the suspect devices, and separated the charge and the detonator from the timer and power pack. The Anti-Terrorist Branch exhibits officer was also in attendance, as if by magic; and had started to bag all the offending items. The local duty officer commented that he was so impressed by such a rapid response from all the emergency services. The observation van drove away when the bomb squad explosive officer confirmed that he had made safe all the suspect devices.

At 5am, the press arrived at the cordons, and were told that a number of explosive devices had been removed from the area of Duckett's Common.

At 6am, a number of police officers, from the bomb search team appeared, and an intense search was made of the area, watched from behind cordons, by a larger contingent of the press.

At 9am, all the breakfast TV news programmes carried stories of an incident at Duckett's Common, where a number of bombs had been located, just prior to a pro-Palestinian demonstration, which was due to take place there. The underground station was closed, and buses diverted. The cider drinker, was arrested, and taken to Hornsey Police Station, where the team of 'Operation Spider' quickly established he had not seen anything strange, and could not remember much about anything. He was given a breakfast and held in custody, till the Doctor said he was sober enough to be released.

At 12noon, Commander Parry was interviewed on TV, and confirmed that due to the vigilance of local police, and their quick action, a major catastrophe had been averted. He said that a number of explosive devices, set to go off when a pro-Palestinian demonstration was due to take place, had been found, and defused. He praised the bravery of the Bomb Squad Officer. He said that had the devices exploded, there would have been wholesale carnage. When questioned as to who was responsible, he said that police were following a number of leads, and it was far too early in the investigation to comment.

The press speculation ran riot, theories surrounding Neo Nazi groups, who had been active in Scandinavia putting bombs down at left wing demonstrations, Jewish extremist groups, and extreme Islamic groups such as the 'Fist of Islam,' who could be engaged in a power struggle with the PLO. The headlines of the tabloids, prepared for the late editions, carried such words as "miracle," "callous" "outrage avoided," and appropriately "cynical politics endanger life."

The 'cider drinker' was interviewed and asked if he had seen anyone place the devices. He said he had not, and had been there nearly all through the night. It transpired he had fallen out with his girlfriend, and had decided to get 'blitzed'.

The 'Fist of Islam' and particularly, Abu Salem, were less than impressed by events.

'How the hell, did they discover them so quick?' said a furious Abu Salem.

'The students could have been spotted. The devices were found just over an hour after they were placed, but why didn't the Police arrest them, if that was the case?' said Magib.

'Do you think Roderick tipped off the Police?' asked Abou.

'He was asking for more money and he threatened us. That does not go with him being a police informer, he was just in it to make money. He would not care if the devices went off or not. I think he was dead, when the information would have been available. He could have told the students, and they could have told the police, but why would they actually then plant the devices. This does not make sense,' said Abu Salem.

'The police said the devices were set to go off during the demonstration, so Rory did his job,' said Magib.

'It would appear so. This has messed up the plans, unless we make the claim now. It will show our intent at least,' mused Abu Salem.

An hour later Reuters in Paris received a claim from the 'Fist of Islam.' The call was traced to the house of Abdullah Ibrahim, in England.

The long-distance camera trained on the Ibrahim's house recorded the photograph of a man, later identified as Abu Salem talking to two men, clearly of Middle East origin, posing as gardeners. They did very little gardening, and were assumed to be sentinels. During the surveillance two other men had been photographed, their photos were sent to Jerusalem and all five men proved to be members of 'The Fist of Islam.'

The team of 'Operation Spider,' gathered to discuss the events, and settle on the next course of action.

'I am sure the group will now ditch our students Hilda and Pete, do you think we can get anything useful from them,' asked Dave Deaney.

'Not any more than we know already. You can bet the

group, particularly Abu Salem, will show their displeasure at the turn of events. He could well take his frustration out on those students,' said Helen.

'Well, the group could still use Roderick, and get him to do something, after all he has been the only one of the students, to have direct contact with them,' said Michael.

'I wouldn't be so sure, they may consider him to be a liability, he is not motivated, like the others. They must have worked out that his priority is money. If they are going to turn on the students, he would be the first one. By the way, has anyone seen, or heard of him, recently?' asked Fred.

The team all shook their heads. 'I agree with Fred here, they are not stupid, our Roderick could well, at this minute, be lying in a ditch somewhere,' said Dave Deaney.

'So, do we think the students will be vulnerable, will they try to get rid of them, and, what about Rory, Maria and Habib?' asked Helen.

'That would be a tall order. I don't think that is an option for them, at this moment, and it will make them vulnerable, if they tried. They can't know what we know about them, and it would be time consuming. Time is what they don't have,' said Michael.

'I agree, I can't see them going after, all of them. The Boss's TV broadcast, said the devices would function during the demo, and that will have gone a long way to show Habib and Rory acted as they had been ordered,' said Fred.

'Hilda and Pete must be vulnerable, the group will have lingering suspicions of what Roderick may have told them, surely,' said Helen.

'They could try and silence them. This could be an opportunity, for us to engage in a little deception. Let us arrest Hilda and Pete, at first the group will not be sure, if the reason for the arrest is, because they were just setting up the demo, or because they were arrested before. Let the press at that point speculate. Then at a suitable moment, if the Boss goes on TV again, he could say they were seen on CCTV, we have the van and pictures of them placing the devices. The group when they hear that, will have two alternatives, as I see it. They could speed up their operation with Mohammed, or abandon everything and run for the hills,' suggested Fred, 'the key is Mohammed.'

'We have averted one disaster, but the other one, Mohammed, is more difficult to avoid, as we don't have him under control. What we now know is where the group is based, the Ibrahim's place. We must presume, Mohammed will go to them there, to get the explosive belt, unless he has it already. Do we know where it is?' asked DI Deaney.

'No, is the simple answer, and we don't know where he is at present, though we know where he sleeps, which is a key surveillance point, and he has not been seen there for hours. The last contact was, when he was seen heading towards the Ibrahim's place. He was lost there, and could be inside. We have the place covered, so we should see if he leaves,' said Michael.

'We should keep a watch on Habib, Rory and Maria as well, as they are the people he could go to for advice, or comfort now, he must be feeling very vulnerable, especially after the group made those threats against his family,' said Helen.

'Agreed, so what is the plan,' asked DI Deaney. 'The top priority is, stop Mohammed blowing himself up.'

'And arresting the group, which is all assembled nicely at the Ibrahim's place,' added Michael.

'The trouble is, they have been so good at distancing themselves from all the operations. We could end up with no actual evidence, against them, unless, they have weapons and explosives at the Ibrahim's place, and we don't know for sure that they do, and you can bet, that Abu Salem will make one of the group members a scape goat, or Ibrahim, and he will walk free,' said Dave Deaney. 'I can't see Hilda and Pete helping much, as they only know what Roderick has fed them, and we don't know where Roderick is. If we can get hold of him, I am sure he would talk.'

'If Mohammed goes to Rory and Maria, we will hear what he says, and if he has control of the suicide belt, we must act,' said Helen. 'The saving of life is a priority.'

'He won't say anything, if we arrest him, as he has the group's threat hanging over him. However, it will mean, we will have to use all the surveillance tapes,' said Michael.

'That will be a nightmare at court,' said Dave Deaney, 'you were the ones to put the bugs in, without any legal authority to do so. They could be ruled out of evidence.'

'Yes, I forgot you British play cricket,' said Michael.

'So, let us recap,' said DI Deaney. 'If Mohammed is seen at the Ibrahim's house, with Abu Salem there, we must pounce, as we will have all the main players there in one place. This will be critical, as we get close to the date of the meeting. We may not get a second chance, as we know the group will try to get out of the country, when they know the plan is set. We, just use what evidence we find.'

'Agreed,' says Michael and the team nod in unison.

'We implement the plan, to switch the hotel the PLO are using,' said Fred.

'Agreed,' was the reply in unison.

'At the moment, we keep the electronic surveillance going on the students, and Rory and Maria's flats, in case Mohammed contacts them,' said Dave Deaney. Depending on what we hear, we arrest Hilda and Pete. If he contacts Habib, we take it he will inform you, Michael.'

'Agreed.'

'Habib, Rory and Maria have made this whole thing a great deal easier for us, by altering those timers. We put their arrest as a low priority, and we do not stop Rory and Maria going to Spain. If anyone screams, we know where they will be, and we can say they will be picked up at a later date. We do not want the group to know, what they did, as they may exact revenge, at some future date,' said Fred. 'We can't use Habib in court, and we will have to keep all that side of the operation secret, in view of possible legal complications.'

'Agreed.'

'So we have a plan, yes,' said Michael. 'As the time gets closer, the group will have to show their hand, and we have to be ready to act quickly. It is going to be a tricky few days, to say the least?'

The electronic surveillance at the students flat activated

and the listeners heard Hilda and Pete discuss the day's events.

'They must have known,' said Hilda, 'how did they find the boxes so quick, and how did they know what they were, it was a uniform PC from the local nick who found them. It couldn't have been that drunk, the one singing in the rain, who told him, surely?'

'No, it could just have been, just chance, the PC who found them, was an ex-marine. The wrong pig, sniffing around, at the wrong moment,' said Pete. 'It could have been that Rory or Habib told them, I never really trusted them.'

'The news said the bombs were going off at the time of the demonstration. Oh God, just think about that, it could have been us. Remember, Rory said, he could not say, exactly, when they were due to go off, as the group set the timers going,' said Hilda. 'We could just have had a lucky escape.'

'He also said nothing would happen, the Police would be bound to find them, how did he know?' said Pete.

'Do you think he was a police informant all along?' suggested Hilda.

'Not sure, if they were going off during the demo, and were set to, why were we allowed to place them, if he was an informant? None of this makes sense,' said Pete.

'What do we do if the group come here, and accuse us of being informants?' said Hilda.

'We will have to try, and off load the blame, on Rory,' said Pete.

The conversation was relayed to the team, and the

decision to arrest Hilda and Pete was brought forward.

The time, was just before midnight, the couple had consumed two bottles of red wine, and were in bed. A steel battering ram shattered the flat door, and police dressed in black, with torches attached to their firearms, swarmed into the bedroom. The couple were unable to react, speechless with terror. They were forced to dress, and were conveyed directly to the secure unit at Paddington Police Station.

DI Deaney and DC Driscoll interviewed them. At first they denied having anything to do with the bombs, until they were confronted with images of them working from the little blue van, and Pete was seen placing one of the devices inside a lamppost. They immediately wanted to speak to their parents, and arrange legal representation.

This was agreed, however, they did not stop talking. They admitted they put the devices in place, but it was only designed as a gesture in support of the Palestinian cause. They had been assured, no one would be hurt, and that they realised, now, they could have been victims. They said they had nothing to do with the manufacture of the bombs. The bombs were made by Rory, who said there would be no problem as they would be found, and Roderick was the person to get the explosives.

It was put to them, that they had no intention of going to the demonstration, after all, they obviously did not trust Rory, and that they were not truly supportive of the political solution of the Palestinian crisis, and supported the more radical approach of the 'Fist of Islam' group, and were prepared to carry out their military action for them.

They were asked to identify the group members. They denied ever having any contact with the group. They said all the communication with the group was through Roderick. Hilda was now in tears and both realised that they could be facing a long prison term.

They were asked who Roderick, Rory, Maria, and Habib were. They said they had no real idea. They said Roderick was a fellow student, as was Habib, though he was a science graduate. They denied knowing who Mohammed was, and where he was likely to be.

'Do you know, what the group are asking him to do'? asked Dave Deaney.

'No,' said Hilda.

'You must have some idea,' countered Deaney.

'We were worried he was a suicide bomber, and tried to stop him. He was very religious, to the point of obsession, we tried to persuade him not to throw his life away,' said Hilda, clearly stressed.

'Did he give you any idea, what the target was?' asked Deaney.

'I don't think he knew, they had not told him,' said Hilda, in tears.

'Are you saying, he was conned into doing the bombing.'

'Yes, in the same way that we were,' said Hilda.

'Who is they?'

'The 'Fist of Islam' I assume, they are not singing from the same hymn sheet as the PLO. If the PLO agreed to the deal with the Israelis, there would be no real free Palestine,' she said, her head in her hands.

'So the target was the meeting?'

'We don't know,' said Hilda.

'You say, you got your instructions from Roderick, where is he now?'

'We don't know, and, we don't know where he came from each time he visited us,' said Pete.

'Do you know if Roderick was a member of the 'Fist of Islam'?'

'He could have become a convert, but we really don't know,' said Pete. At this point they said they were not going to say anymore, until their lawyer arrived.

Helen and Fred went to see Habib. Fred introduced Helen as an Israeli police officer, and told him that they knew his story, and were aware of the part he played in seeing that the devices planted by Hilda and Pete did not work, and the role Rory and Maria played to the same end.

'They could not bear to see more innocent lives, wrecked by people who just had their own political agenda. Like me, they have concluded the armed struggle, for whatever cause, is pointless, and is conducted by so many unscrupulous men, just after money or power,' said Habib. 'We have all been caught up in events, we had no control over, and at last we had the opportunity to break free from this terror.'

'We are truly grateful, for what you all have done, but that is not the whole problem, as you know,' said Fred. 'Do you have any idea where Mohammed is? And what his intention is?'

'He has some form of suicide attack in mind, we think it'll be a vest,' said Habib 'all three of us have tried to dissuade him, but he is too damaged, to take any notice of us,

219

I am afraid.'

'Did he say what the target is? asked Fred.

'I don't think he knows for certain,' said Habib 'but I am sure you can work it out, it must be the PLO-Israeli meeting. The PLO leaders will be more vulnerable than the Israeli's, who have very strong security.'

'Has he hinted, in any way, as to how he will deliver the device?' asked Fred.

'Sorry, no,' said Habib. 'I wish I knew, and could do something to save him wasting his life.'

Helen explained 'I knew him as a childhood friend, we played together in my father's olive groves, as many children, we did not differentiate between Jew and Arab.'

'As did many children then,' said Habib.

'Would Rory or Maria know where he is now?' asked Fred.

'I don't know,' said Habib.

'Do you know where they are?' asked Fred.

'I have an idea, do you just want to chat to them?' said Habib. 'Or arrest them?'

'Our priority is to find Mohammed, time is running out, as you must be aware, and we want to stop him killing himself and others,' said Helen with some feeling.

'You still like him, don't you,' said Habib.

'Yes, I have tried to talk to him, but he has changed so much, I barely recognised him,' said Helen, 'do you think Rory and Maria, will know, any clue will be of help, seriously, do you think we could talk to them?'

'They could still be at the flat, they are planning to run,' said Habib.

'Can you talk to them for us,' asked Helen.

'I can try,' said Habib, 'I can see what their reaction is.'

'Tell them we are indebted to them, for what they did, in saving all those students at that demo, but for their intervention, there would have been a real tragedy, which would have left so many either injured, or dead,' said Fred. 'I can't say anything definite, but as far as I am concerned, here and now, there are political moves to draw a line under many of the events, that occurred in Ireland and Spain, and it would serve no purpose to rake up old muck, especially when we have the opportunity, to save one life, and possibly many others.'

'Ok, I will try, where will you be?' said Habib.

'Outside the flat in a car,' said Fred.

They took Habib to the flat, and he went in. He told Rory and Maria not to panic, but an Anti-Terrorist detective and an Israeli police officer, a lady, were outside and wanted an unofficial chat with them.

'If they had wanted to arrest you, they would have just stormed the flat, they are desperate to save Mohammed, and the Israeli, is a childhood friend of his,' said Habib.

'We are about to go,' said Maria. 'We don't want to be stopped now, it's our only chance of breaking free of these recurring nightmares.'

'They know that, they have said they will not stop you,' said Habib.

'We don't know where he is, we all know is how this could end, in a situation where they can do nothing, but shoot him,' said Rory.

'We tried everything we could, to stop him, do they

221

know that?' said Maria.

'Yes, they know, they want any clue as to where he may be, how he is to link up with the 'Fist of Islam' people, to get the vest, and what the ultimate target is,' said Habib.

'We can't answer those questions, in so many ways I wish we could,' said Maria, 'if we did, we would tell them, what shall we say, Rory?'

'Ok Habib, Mohammed came here an hour ago, we were talking to him when one of the group came, and took him away, we don't know where. He said we would not get any more money, and, if we stayed around any longer, the same thing that happened to Roderick, would happen to us,' said Rory.

'Do you know where they took him?' asked Habib.

'No, but Mohammed slipped us a card, it's a business card, 'Middle East Oil Company,' and when we looked out of the window, he was getting into one of their vans, it had their name on its side,' said Rory.

'Right let me tell the officers, I'll be back. How long ago was that?' 'Less than ten minutes,' said Maria.

Habib ran down the stairs and up to the car, Fred and Helen got out. Habib quickly told them, what he had been told. Helen relayed it straight back to DI Deaney.

'He must have slipped away from the Ibrahim's place, and no one saw him, not even us! The group would have been desperate, to get him back, and realised this is where he would go,' she paused and pointed.

'Is that Rory and Maria?' said Fred indicating the couple leaving the building.

'Yes, what are you going to do?' asked Habib anxiously.

'Relax, I just want to say goodbye,' said Fred.

Fred called out 'please just a minute, I won't delay you, as I know you have a train to catch. I just wanted to thank you for what you did.' The couple paused and turned.

'Rory, can I just say I think a career change to being a shepherd would be a good move, as I hear you don't have much future as an electronics engineer,' Fred said with a smile.

Rory hesitated and then said, 'you might be right at that.'

Maria laughed and said, 'thank you, but we do have a train to catch, it was nice to meet you, and I only wish, it was not under such circumstances.'

'I understand, I too have little time, I have a young man, to save from himself,' said Fred.

'Oh, please do, he is a total innocent, in a wicked world, caught up like us, in a tangled web of deceit,' said Maria.

'I will try my best,' said Fred.

'I know you will, and we do hope you succeed,' said Rory.

With that the couple continued down the road towards the underground station. Habib came up behind Fred.

'I am glad you did that,' he said.

'Did what, Habib?' said Fred with a smile.

'Yes, I suppose some people will criticise you if they found out, but they won't find out from me,' said Habib. 'Common sense has triumphed for once, I think.'

They learnt from DI Deaney that a company van was seen to enter the grounds of the Ibrahim's mansion. A slim figure was escorted out of the back of the van and taken

223

into the house. It could only have been Mohammed, and the time of the direct journey from the flat to the mansion, confirmed their suspicions.

The plan to change the hotel the PLO leaders were due to stay at, was implemented and they were moved out of London, with increased security. However an employee of the original hotel, phoned Abu Salem at the Ibrahim's house to tell him the PLO leaders, would not be staying at his hotel.

Abu Salem screamed down the phone demanding to know where they were to go. His informant did not know the details of the new hotel, no one at the hotel did, he had asked, and was told it was secret.

Abu Salem calls Razak, a group member.

'We have to find out where this new hotel is, and we have no time, get that slut, Fatima, yes, Ibrahim's wife, to get Jones here, on whatever pretext she can manufacture. We have to extract that information from him. Where is Abdullah?'

'He's at the office,' came the reply.

'Ok, that's good, get her to call Jones now, say I want her to seduce him, tell him she is desperate to see him, and, that Abdullah will be away for hours, and keep Abdullah away,' said a furious Abu Salem.

Fatima does as she is bidden, and Jones says he is on his way. He leaves a message with SB Reserve, that he has to go and see a registered informant, who will tell him where the group, the 'Fist of Islam' is. He says he has to go alone, the informant would not talk unless he is alone. With that, after a call to Fatima to say he is on his way, he heads for the Ibrahim's mansion.

The calls to and from the mansion had been monitored. A moments panic results, until DI Deaney confirms that Superintendent Jones, does not know the location of the new hotel.

'Does he know what he is walking into?' asks Michael.

'The idiot has no idea,' says Dave Deaney.

'Should we stop him?' says Michael.

'Why, he is going to see a registered informant,' says Dave Deaney trying to supress a smile.

Chapter 10

لـا ف غ ز ا ئ ك ا ف أ ك ن ر ك] ا ت ح إ لـ

Determination is the key to everything.

"How is Mohammed? Keep him calm, and focused,' says Abu Salem to Razak, his right-hand man.

'Easier said, than done, he is still on about the children of his sister, he does not want them touched. If they are, he won't do anything,' says Razzak.

'Just tell him anything, say that they will be given special care at the camp, where they will be the children of a martyr,' says Abu Salem.

'We still have to give him the final briefing,' says Razzak 'and we don't know where the new hotel is. We'll need to get someone there, to see what the security is like, and at least, the layout of the place.'

'Yes, I know, I am working on that now,' says Abu Salem. 'Continue as planned, he will pose as press. He has the accreditation already, so he will be able to get to the entrance. They will have to go in cars to the meeting, so that is when he can run forward, and activate the device. Every hotel has an entrance, and that is where the chauffeurs will go to pick up any VIP. They won't know, it will be a suicide job, they have never had such an attack here in England before.'

'I think they can guess it could be on the cards, though,' says Razzak.

'It won't matter, even if he is discovered, he will activate the device, the point will be made,' says Salem. 'He is expendable, look, just get him ready, the vest is ready and primed, I take it?'

'Yes, he is seeing to it, at least he knows what to do with that,' says Razzak.

'That's good, he wants to serve Allah, now is his chance,' says Salem.

'He does not stop reciting the Quran, it is driving me mad,' says Razzak.

'Good, make sure he has a good meal, anything he wants, and make sure he does all the rituals, he is bathed and has on his new suit, otherwise he won't go,' says Abu Salem.

'Right, he wanted two copies of books called the "Book of Hadith," Islamic sayings, I have them. Do I give them to him?' asks Razzak.

'Yes, of course,' says Salem impatiently. 'As soon as we have details of the location, we will give him that final briefing. Make a fuss of him, tell him what a hero he will be in the eyes of Allah, any damn thing, just keep him focused.'

'Yes, no problem,' says Razzak.

A slim figure, had paused outside the door, it was Mohammed. He had heard every word.

A few minutes later Razak tells Salem that Jones is on his way to the Mansion.

'Good, brief the others as to what will happen here. We will get the information we need out of Jones, and then dispose of him. Are the cars ready, and the charges set?' asks Salem.

'Yes,' and with that, Razak gathered his team together.

'Once Mohammed has been sent to the target, in the cab. The Ibrahim's will be killed, with Jones the policeman,' said Razak. 'We will empty the safe, Abu has the combination from Fatima. We will use the BMW, and the Porsche, to get away to the farm, where we pick up the Mercedes, and then, we drive to Heathrow, we have open tickets ready. Is that clear.'

'When will the explosives go off here?' asked one of the members.

'I will set them when Mohammed is about to go, that will leave us four hours to get away from the building. They will explode when the police are here, and that will keep them busy, and not worrying about us,' said Razzak.

Jones arrived at the mansion, and was met by Fatima, dressed in an almost transparent flowing robe. She embraces him and steers him towards a bedroom, where she laid down with him. As they lay on the bed, she stroked his hair. She confided in him, that she has always wanted to meet Nasser Fatah, the leader of the PLO Delegation, and asks if he can arrange it for her. Jones tells her, that this is definitely not the time, in view of the upcoming meeting. Security would be so tight, they would not let, even her, in to see him.

'Oh, but I am sure, I could persuade them to let me in, we pour enough money into his coffers' she smiles and looks into his eyes. 'My friend at the Grosvenor, says he is not there anymore, where is he?'

'I can't tell you, Fatima,' he says.

'It's just, that you won't,' she says in a loud voice, which is the signal for Abu Salem to enter followed by Abdullah Ibrahim her husband.

'Fatima, I hope you enjoyed yourself, the video is going to be a sensation,' said Abu Salem with a laugh.

'You disgust me!' choked Abdullah? 'How could you, Fatima, with this man?'

'Oh, this is not the first time, we have a whole series of videos and photos, for the press, and for you Abdullah. You can see what a slut she truly is,' said Salem laughing.

'Fatima, why?' cried Abdullah.

'I did it for Allah, for the 'Fist of Islam,' do you think, I got any enjoyment out of it, she said truculently. 'I have sacrificed my honour for the cause, for Allah?'

Jones rose, halfway from the sheets, white as the sheets he lay on. A realisation of the situation, immediately dawning on him.

'You won't get away with this,' he said in a hoarse whisper.

'There is nothing you can do Superintendent, except tell us where the PLO are staying now,' demanded Salem.

'No, I can't, won't and I don't know,' said Jones.

'But you are the Superintendent in charge of the Middle

East desk at Special Branch, or that is what you told Fatima. So, tell us. You must know,' said Salem in a mocking voice.

'I said, I don't know,' said Jones.

'Now, if Razak here, puts a bullet in your leg, and then one in your groin, will that help you to remember?' said Salem.

'I don't know, we don't arrange these things, it is the Diplomatic Protection Group who do,' said Jones, trying to remain calm.

'Ok, now if you don't cooperate, we will put those bullets in you, and then ensure your memory is kept alive through the videos. Razak on my count of three, one....' shouted Salem.

'Wait, they are going to the 'White Hart Hotel' near Hertford,' said Jones in a panic.

'Now, that was not so difficult, was it? You will be kept here, till we confirm what you say. It is lucky, it is just down the road,' said Salem.

'Razak tie his hands, we will deal with him later. Mr Jones please take a seat for now, Fatima I am sure will look after you. Razak make sure they do not leave the room. That includes you Abdulla, I am sure you have much to discuss with Fatima,' said Salem with a smile.

The observation post hidden in the undergrowth outside the mansion, had recorded Jones entering the building.

SB reserve confirmed that Jones had gone to see a registered informant, looking for information about the group, and that he went alone. Commander SB was contacted, and made enquiries to ascertain how much he knew. It was soon established, that he had been asking about the final arrangements for the conference, and details of where the PLO leaders, were staying.

SB had told him that the Diplomatic Group were handling the arrangements. He contacted the DPG, who stone walled him, however, he found a young member of their support staff, and bullied him into saying where the change in venue was. An SB detective constable, who was with him, thought it very odd he did not know, and had to resort to making enquiries with the DPG. When he heard that his commander was asking how much Jones knew of the arrangements, the detective put two and two together, and informed the commander of what had happened. Commander SB promptly informed Commander Parry of the development.

Commander Parry immediately passed the information on to his team on the ground, and left to join them.

On arrival a few minutes later, the commander said 'We now know Jones knows about the change of hotel. It is time we wrapped this up. We have the 'Fist of Islam' group, and Mohammed bottled up here at the Ibrahim's place. So Mr Deaney, put the firearms team on red alert, and, Dave, I want you and Fred to go in behind them, and you too Helen. I do not know how you feel, but if he has a device on his person, will you try talking to him, and persuade him not to arm it, and then blow himself up. I am pretty sure he knows, he has been conned into doing all this for Salem by now, and not Allah? If we think it is armed, you are not to go near him. If the opportunity arises, this will be done at distance to keep you as safe as we can. There is a limit to who, or what, we can risk to save this young man, from himself. The firearms team have been briefed, and will not hesitate, if the situation demands.'

'Yes, that will be fine sir,' said Helen.

As the team arrived in the mansion grounds, a cab was stopped entering the main gates. The driver said he had come to collect a Mohammed Ali, and take him to the White Hart Hotel in Hertford.

'That means Mohammed will have the explosive vest on, and they have just been waiting for this cab to collect him, once they know he is on his way, to the target, they will kill Jones for sure, and most likely the Ibrahim couple too,' said Helen.

'Right, Dave, give the Firearms Team the green light, we have to go!' ordered the commander.

'Ron, its go, go!' yelled Dave Deaney to the firearms inspector.

'Go, Go, Go!' yelled the inspector into his radio, and his team streamed across the lawns, emerged from outbuildings and the undergrowth.

'The suicide bomber must be ready. He will not have armed it to travel, surely. What does the cabbie say?' asked Dave Deaney.

'He's just from the local cab firm, he is not involved. He has been scooped up, and taken to the local nick. He just says he came to collect a fare, to the hotel, and we know he has not seen Mohammed, and does not know about the vest. We will talk to him later if that is ok. He is scared stiff, and totally confused,' said DC Driscoll.

There were several loud bangs, as the Police entered the

building, followed by a short exchange of gunfire. A group member was killed, and a firearms PC was injured.

The main focus of attention, was immediately centred on the large reception room on the ground floor, which doubled as a ballroom. The firearms unit, aware that there was a suicide bomber amongst the terrorist group, went in hard to stop him arming the device. The 'flash bangs' temporarily stunned the occupants, a group member on the door dropped his weapon, and was grabbed by the firearms team, who dragged him outside, to lie flat on the lawn.

Inside the ballroom, as smoke cleared, Abu Salem could be seen getting to his feet, holding a submachine gun, pointed at Superintendent Jones, Razak also armed with a similar weapon was pointing it at the Ibrahim's, while Mohammed, who had got to his feet with some difficulty, stood close to them. All the people at the end of the room had red dots on their torsos, from the lasers on the firearms team's weapons.

'Drop the weapons, keep your hands where we can see them,' shouted the firearms team leader. He could see Mohammed was standing with his arms out, palms towards him, so held his fire.

'Come any further and he detonates the bomb,' shouted Abu Salem, 'the superintendent and my friends here, will all die.'

Mohammed, who clearly had not read the script said, 'It's Allah's will, that we all will die for his glory.'

'We the 'Fist of Islam' soldiers, have more of Allah's work to do, tell the police gunmen to get back, or we shoot this pig. Get someone here we can negotiate with, we want cars to the airport, and a plane on standby, fuelled to go now, or these people will die,' demanded Salem.

'You're in no position to dictate anything Salem,' was the reply from DI Deaney.

'For God's sake, do as they say, and no one will get hurt' screamed an agitated Jones.

'Order them to withdraw,' said Salem to Jones.

'He is in no position to order anything. We have the whole house surrounded, your fellow terrorists, have been rounded up, there is nowhere for you to go,' said Deaney.

'Then you will die too, and have the blood of these people on your hands,' hissed Salem.

'Abu why do you turn on us? We are your friends, we supported your cause. You are my lover, you know I will do anything for you. Why, why?' sobbed Fatima.

'We have supported you, financed you, housed and cared for you,' said Abdullah Ibrahim.

'And now your job is done, you have both served your purpose' said Abu Salem, 'Mohammed if they move closer, or a shot is fired, release the bomb trigger. If you shoot at him, he will release the switch, he will hold it open, kill him, and he releases it, and the bomb goes off. Do you understand?'

Mohammed did not move or alter his stance his hands away from the bomb and visible.

'Mohammed listen to me, this is not Allah's wish, that man is doing all this for himself, he is not a true believer, he is just using you,' said Helen emerging from behind a firearms officer, who remained pointing a weapon down the room at Abu Salem.

'Don't listen to that Israeli bitch, they are the cause of all our problems, they are the arch enemy of Allah, of Islam,' spat out Abu Salem.

'Mohammed, you will give up your life, for no good reason, this man only seeks power for himself, come to me, you know me, you can trust me, we have been friends all of our lives, surely that counts for something?' she pleaded.

Mohammed with tears running down his face said quietly 'Helen sweet girl, please go from here, please, I have to do what Allah is telling me to do. You know that, it will be for the best, trust me.'

'Oh Mohammed, this does not have to end this way, here, in bloodshed, you can speak for Islam, without killing anyone, it will have far more impact than this,' she pleaded.

'Mohammed do as I say, we don't have much time. There are bombs ticking down as we speak. They are all over the house, and will bring the building down, and, no one will get out alive, and, you Israeli bitch, you will be a martyr for Islam too. I want a closed van, to take us to Stanstead, the Ibrahims and Jones, will come as hostages. Do as I say, now, or you will all die,' said Abu Salem

'We are all the sons of Allah, Abu, we are here to glorify his name,' said Mohammed quietly as he moved steadily towards Abu Salem.

'No,' he yelled, 'I am the leader of his army, the 'Fist of Islam,' do as I say. It is his wish, I have more work to do. You can glorify his name, Mohammed.' The occupants of the room froze, and stared at Mohammed, as he calmly kept walking towards Abu Salem, along a path between him and the firearms policeman, his hands out from the device still.

'You too, are only here to glorify his name Abu Salem – Allah Akbar, Maa Shora Allah,' – and, with that he moved suddenly, taking all unawares, throwing himself against the leader of the 'Fist of Islam.'

Abu Salem tried to turn his gun on him, and instinctively fired hitting Jones who collapsed on the floor, just as there was a large flash and bang. Most of the explosion was contained between the two bodies.

The Ibrahims were thrown against the wall, collapsing in a heap. Jones groaned, tried to rise, and collapsed. Black smoke filled the room which fell silent, before more of the firearms team streamed into the room.

A cloud of charred burning paper, containing Arabic writing, started to rain down around them. Razak tried to rise, before the gun was kicked away from his feet, where he had dropped it. He was grabbed and flattened.

Dave Deaney, Fred, and Helen had been thrown to the floor by the blast. They picked themselves up, and Dave Deaney slightly dazed brushed the burning pieces of paper from his clothes. There were cries for 'medics' and 'ambulances.'

'What the hell is this stuff?' asked Dave Deaney.

'Arabic religious text,' said Helen through tears, as she stared at the disfigured form of her Arab friend.

The medical staff started to care for the Ibrahims and Jones, who had been injured by the blast. Razak pleaded for help, and for forgiveness, and, then started swearing in Arabic.

'Well Mohammed got his wish to die for Allah, and he took Salem with him, but I don't believe Salem was so willing to go,' remarked Dave Deaney.

'We still have to find these devices,' said Fred quietly, 'we must get everyone out of here, and quick, and get a search team ready. Get the Expo here with the receiver device. We can only hope that the timers on these devices, are all the ones Habib and Rory made.'

'Yes Fred, I am here,' said the Explosives Officer from behind him, 'and you can operate this tracker device for me, I think we should be the only ones, to be here though, the search team can come in, when you have electronically swept. Let us find a device quick, and see if it has the safe timers in it. If not we will have to go to a plan B and quick.'

They started systematically to search the building, and it was not long before they found a device, in a ground floor room.

The little transmitter on the circuit board sent a reassuring signal to the receiver Fred held, and, he secretly blessed Habib and Rory, as the explosive charge was a sizeable one. In all, five more devices were found around the building, all gave a response on the receiver scanner.

The timers had all been marked for four hours, so it was decided to leave the building empty for another four hours before the Forensic Team went in.

'We just can't take any chances,' said the Explosives Officer.

It transpired that Mohammed had removed at least two of three charges from his belt, and surrounded the remaining charge, with religious text from the Quran and the book of Hadith. This substantially cut down the potential collateral damage, that would have occurred, if he had detonated the full charge.

On hearing this Dave Deaney said, 'well he certainly spread the word of Allah, I just wish he had done it, in a more conventional way.'

The forensic search conducted at the flat of Hilda and Pete, provided forensic links to the timed devices encountered. They were eventually charged with assisting in terrorist acts.

The meeting between the PLO leaders and the Israelis went ahead without any further drama. The press speculated that the raid on the Ibrahim's mansion, was related to the meeting, but, police refused to confirm or deny the speculation, that was until the meeting had concluded. The press said that the arrest of the hard core of the 'Fist of Islam' would mean that the free world could breathe a sigh of relief.

Secretly Habib was praised for his role in the affair, and in the subsequent enquiry, it was agreed his part in the operation should be kept secret to ensure that there would be no reprisals against any of his family, still in the Lebanon. He spoke up for Rory and Maria and said their role in the affair had been crucial for its safe outcome. He also confirmed that they had left their flat, just before, Fred and Helen arrived there.

Months later an unofficial meeting with the Guardia Civil in Spain, resulted in them confirming that Rory was living with Maria at Uncle Luigi's farmhouse, and was tending his sheep once more. The Spanish police were told of the part the couple played in avoiding wholesale carnage in London. They said they would keep an eye on them. Maria was of no interest to them now, as there was speculation about an amnesty for ETA activists. So Rory, now, known as Raoul Gonzales, settled down to a peaceful, rural existence. The Spanish police said they would protect the couple from any more marauding Arabs.

Habib went on to become a lecturer in electronic engineering at the university. Razak got life imprisonment at his trial, and the other members of the 'Fist of Islam,' got thirty years for offences which included the murder of Roderick. Superintendent Jones resigned and took early retirement.

Commander Parry thanked Helen publicly for her role in the investigation, and her courage in the final scene. Before she went back to Jerusalem he saw Helen and Fred together. 'Well done you were both thrown into a difficult situation, and handled it well. It is good to see our two forces working together, and trusting each other to do the right thing. After all the preservation of innocent lives, must be the priority of all nations. The full story can never be told. On balance I am glad that you were just too late, to arrest Rory and Maria. I just hope he can stay clean until this Good Friday agreement comes into force. I understand the Spanish think the same way about Maria. It's just a shame we could not thank them for their part in doctoring those timers, that certainly made life for us a lot easier.'

'Yes Sir, such a shame,' said Fred keeping a straight face and Helen could not resist a smile, as the commander looked at them with narrowed eyes. He nodded, smiled, and said, 'I thought so.'

When they were alone, Fred said to Helen 'it was sad your little friend went that way, he clearly saw through Salem at the end. We can only hope his sacrifice was not in vain, and the world will become a more peaceful and safer place.'

'Amen to that Fred,' said Helen.

Fred took Helen to the airport. 'It has been lovely seeing you again Helen, it was a 'tangled web' we had to unravel, and boy did it have its scary moments, but it got sorted in the end, and that is the main thing,' he said.

She gave him a peck on the cheek, 'it's always fun working with you Fred, now you must come to Jerusalem, promise now.'

'I promise, Helen.'

With that she strode away down towards the El Al.